THIS
IS NOT
THE
REAL
WORLD

THIS IS NOT THE REAL WORLD

ANNA CAREY

QUIRK BOOKS

PHILADELPHIA

Text copyright © 2022 by Anna Carey
Cover illustration copyright © 2022 by Silke Werzinger

Library of Congress Cataloging-in-Publication Data
Names: Carey, Anna, author. | Carey, Anna. This is not the Jess Show.
Title: This is not the real world / Anna Carey.
Description: Philadelphia : Quirk Books, [2022] | Audience: Ages 14 and up. | Summary: "After months of living in the outside world, Jess Flynn returns to the reality show she was unknowingly trapped in for most of her life to expose the dark truth about the production company behind the show"—Provided by publisher.
Identifiers: LCCN 2021053545 (print) | LCCN 2021053546 (ebook) | ISBN 9781683692812 (hardcover) | ISBN 9781683692829 (ebook)
Subjects: CYAC: Reality television programs—Fiction. | Secrets—Fiction. | Family life—Fiction. | LCGFT: Novels.
Classification: LCC PZ7.C21 Tj 2022 (print) | LCC PZ7.C21 (ebook) | DDC [Fic]—dc23
LC record available at https://lccn.loc.gov/2021053545
LC ebook record available at https://lccn.loc.gov/2021053546

ISBN: 978-1-68369-281-2

Printed in the United States of America

Typeset in Univers, Sabon, and Kindness Matters

Designed by Elissa Flanigan
Production management by John J. McGurk

Quirk Books
215 Church Street
Philadelphia, PA 19106
quirkbooks.com

10 9 8 7 6 5 4 3 2 1

TO EVERYONE AT WWHS,
NOW AND THEN

1

The gondola glided between buildings, and that same song filtered in right as we slipped under the third arched bridge. It was coming from an upper balcony, where the same violin player sat, his bow gliding back and forth across the strings. Below him, the window was open, and the same man with that same stubby gray mustache was cooking pasta. It wasn't until Kipps pointed it out that I realized he looked exactly like Chef Boyardee. He even had the white hat.

"How much do you think they paid for that product placement?" I asked.

"This is supposed to be romantic, Jess."

I tried not to look at Kipps too much in the simulations, because his features were always a little off from what they were in real life. His nose looked huge and angular, his wavy hair like tiny brown snakes spilling out of his scalp. His left eye always went rogue. Sometimes I wasn't sure if he was looking at me or my right ear.

"But seriously. Italy, the association with the Venice canals and pasta. I bet that spot was as pricey as the Armani one." I pointed to the right but I was a beat early. The gondola took a few seconds to clear the end of the building and then we saw the dark-haired couple dancing in the alley, their cheeks pressed together. In an instant the woman stepped out, spinning once under the man's arm, then pausing to show the long, lacy black skirt to us. "Or maybe that's better real estate. It's more front and center."

The violin music faded behind us, giving way to the sounds of tourists shopping for watercolors on the bridge above. An American woman with overlined lips argued with the seller over two euros. Kipps squeezed my hand, then the scene stopped and the menu came down in front of us. VENICE, ITALY, was highlighted.

"What are you doing?"

"You're not into it. Maybe Singapore?" He flicked through the list of cities, past Tokyo and Marrakech. We'd already been to Paris five times. "What about Siem Reap? We could do the hot-air balloon over Angkor Wat again."

"Eh."

"Eh?!? It's one of the wonders of the world."

"We've been to all of these places already. It's just . . . the same thing again and again. We must've gone down this canal a dozen times, and we've played Bot Wars and explored every corner of the Spiderverse and did that stupid building game—"

"I like Skyscrapers."

"It's just okay."

"It could be worse. At least we're together."

I tried to look at Kipps, but his eye was rebelling again. I knew he was right—we were lucky—so I kissed him. Our VR goggles clinked against each other and we pulled them off, leaving the world behind.

The immersive theater in Charli and Sara's house was all black—black walls and black ceiling and black foam floor. Monochrome props in varying states of disarray. With the lights dimmed everything blended together, and it felt like we were floating in space, weightless, suspended in a dream. Kipps's hand slid from my cheek to my neck as we kissed, then out across my collarbone. Whatever was missing in Venice was here, as I drew him closer, his mouth against mine.

He fell back onto the floor and I rested my face in his neck, listening to his breaths slow, then steady. I kicked at the padded gondola seat that came in the World in a Box, pushing it away from us. The scaffolding platform from Skyscrapers rested against the wall beside the lights from the Thai beach experience, which were so strong you had to wear sunblock.

"Don't expect me to feel too sorry for you," he said, squeezing my arm. "I mean, how bad is it, really? Being stuck here with a devastatingly handsome, *younger* man—"

"Eleven months. You're only eleven months younger."

"Still . . . you have your own personal love machine, catering to your every whim."

"Ew. Please do not refer to yourself as a love machine."

"Okay, okay. Your devoted boyfriend who loves you."

His head was leaning against mine when he said it, his

eyes staring straight up at the ceiling. I tried to fix my face into something normal, but the words were still with me, and then I couldn't stop smiling. I kept repeating them in my head—*who loves you*—trying to be sure I hadn't imagined it. It was possible he just meant it in a casual way, like how he loved the mango ice cream bars Charli ordered from Delancey Grocer, or the mattress on his bed, which was like a huge block of clay that left Kipps-shaped indents every time he got up.

Your boyfriend who loves you.

Your devoted boyfriend who loves you.

Love.

Love.

Love.

I couldn't tell if he expected me to say it back. He'd closed his eyes and I played with the front pocket of his shirt, running my finger over the stitching. I'd thought through it a hundred times. What would've happened if I hadn't gotten in the car with him that day, when he shouted at me from the driver's seat of the Land Rover. What would've happened if the NextGen Cloud had crapped out on the highway, with hundreds of cars racing past, before we could reach the more secluded spot by the golf course. Like-Life Productions would've found us and taken us back before we even made it to the city. Or if the gun had gone off a few seconds earlier, or I'd lost the book with Sara's number in it?

Kipps was right, even if he didn't mean it that way. We *were* lucky.

As boring as it was sometimes, the house Charli and Sara had built in Maine was its own world, with enough rooms and corners to lose yourself in. It was a Genius Home, an upgrade on the Smart Home, and I sometimes tripped over the machines that scuttled about, sweeping and mopping, or was startled when my favorite song blasted through the bathroom speakers as I turned on the shower. The beach was a short walk through the double gates, and there were woods surrounding the house in every direction. They'd installed an Illusion Fence around the property, which was another tech-y, 2037 invention I'd discovered after leaving Swickley. The delicate screen was like chameleon's skin, blending into the scenery around it, so the woods looked empty, the shoreline uninterrupted. After almost fifteen years of being watched every second of every day, I'd completely disappeared.

"Hey," I said.

Kipps turned, his eyes meeting mine.

"Did you mean that?"

"What?"

"The L-word."

"*The L-word?* When you put it like that—"

"Love. You said you loved me."

Maybe I was a coward, to not say it back right then. Why did I have to think and overthink everything, hesitate and question and worry and not just do the thing, do the brave thing that Kipps always seemed so capable of?

"Of course I meant it," he said, sandwiching my hand between his. "I've never been in love before, but this is it.

ANNA CAREY

Don't you think?"

"Yeah. It definitely feels that way."

It was still new, when he traced his fingers up mine, my skin firing beneath his touch. In the last five months Kipps became less and less an idea and more himself, and I sometimes felt like I was playing catch-up, trying to know him as well as he knew me. We'd sit hidden beneath the dock as he described his old apartment in Pennsylvania, the closet his parents had converted to a bedroom with a full-sized mattress where he and his brother, Reed, slept. He felt guilty that he'd left Reed with no note, no explanation about where he'd gone, even if he'd hated it inside the set and been angry at his parents for forcing him into a lead role. Reed was nineteen, and I vaguely remembered him from Swickley High—he was a junior when we were freshmen. When he'd graduated, so had all the extras who were his age, and even though he had a long-distance boyfriend and friends he talked to online, Kipps was one of the few people he hung out with IRL (an abbreviation Sara had taught me).

Kipps's hair tickled my cheek. Since we'd gotten to Maine it had grown long, a shaggy mess that he tucked behind his ears. Charli didn't know anyone she trusted enough to cut it for him, considering he wasn't supposed to be here—neither of us were. Last month I'd turned eighteen, an event we'd kept referring to as "clearing my birthday" because that's what it had felt like—a hurdle in the distance. Now that I wasn't a minor anymore my parents couldn't take me back to the *Stuck in the '90s* set. Like-Life Productions couldn't legally justify looking for me, though I knew they still were. As the weeks wore on it was Kipps we worried about. Kipps was still seventeen, and the most vulnerable, and the biggest reason we didn't venture out more. It never seemed worth the risk to go far from the house, knowing someone might recognize us. We were always one rando's iPhone photo or livestream away from discovery.

"What are we going to do, stuck here for ten more months?" I said with a smirk, propping my head on my hand so I could look at him. I had ideas . . . we both did. There was only so much time we could spend playing VR games or studying to get our final credits to graduate. Lately we snuck into each other's rooms more and more, our limbs twisted together, Kipps's hands fumbling with the clasp of my bra. We were speeding closer to having sex, to losing our virginity to each other, to doing *it* (a phrase Sara had described as "hopelessly heteronormative"). However you said it, I was starting to understand what the big deal was.

"I don't know." He smiled back. "We'll have to find something."

"Hmmmmm . . ." I put my finger on my chin, pretending to be deep in thought.

We kissed again, but this time I pulled away, standing so we didn't get into it right here, right on the theater floor. It was almost time for dinner, and it was my night to cook. He watched me as I straightened my shorts, a purple denim pair Sara had bought for me online. He watched me as I combed my hair with my fingers and called the lights up, so the room came into focus around us. Then I padded to the door.

I hovered there, watching him watch me, and rested my head on the frame. He rolled over and tucked his arm under his head, as if that last kiss had drained him of his life force.

"Dramatic much?" I asked.

"Always."

"And . . . I love you too," I finally said. "So so so so so much."

I raised my arms, spreading them wide. I love you this much. More than I can actually say.

He threw his head back and covered his heart, as if the words had shot across the room and struck him in the chest. Then he was smiling, and I was smiling, and he turned to me one last time to watch me go.

"Oh, thank you, Jess Flynn," he said, finally prying himself off the floor.

Love, love, love. For some reason, it didn't compare.

My name on his lips was still my favorite sound.

2

Charli poked a charred carrot with her fork. She tried to cut it, but the burnt parts covered the edible parts in a nasty black casing. Instead she set her utensils down and glanced sideways toward the front windows, waiting for the delivery drone.

"It's supposed to taste like cardboard." I broke my chicken breast apart with my fork. "That's what I was going for."

"Chicken à la papyrus." Kipps took a big bite, his eyes wide as he chewed. "Mmmmm . . . delicious."

"I mean," Sara said. "It's better than last time. That pasta was barely cooked. So I say A-plus for improvement, Jess."

"Why, thank you."

The agreement was that Kipps, Sara, and I each made dinner at least one night a week. No one ever said it needed to be edible. Charli had taken on two nights, but even her dishes were usually undercooked or oversalted, and she'd finally confessed that all the homemade soups and lasagnas she'd served us inside the set came from catering trays that were passed through a trapdoor in the back of our oven. Even the fridge had a secret panel. It made sense now why it would suddenly be stocked with Tupperwared leftovers I'd never seen my parents cook.

Charli dragged her finger across her iPhone screen, checking the drone's location. From where I was sitting I saw my mom's name, HELENE HART, appear and disappear as a green text square.

"Ugh, she's texting you again?" I said.

"Wouldn't it be more depressing if she never texted? If she never once asked if I'd heard from you?"

She stood, then practically sprinted to the front steps. As soon as she opened the door we heard the whir of the drone blades, and she turned to the side, blocking us so we wouldn't be caught on the tracking camera. When she came back she was carrying a plastic box filled with dry ice, clouds drifting out of holes in the sides.

"At what point are we going to just order straightaway?" Sara pulled the sushi container out and set it on the table. "We are victims of our own optimism."

"Hey, speak for yourself. I'm a good cook." Kipps plucked a piece of crab roll with his fingers and popped it in his mouth.

"Compared to the rest of us," Sara corrected. "Which isn't saying much."

"Can I look?" I pointed to Charli's phone.

"I'm betting it's the same as last time." She picked up a

piece of salmon roll with one hand and scanned her face with the other, unlocking the screen. Then she slid it over to me.

My mom had checked in with Charli almost every month for the last five months, even though they were technically supposed to hate each other. Mostly she said just that: *Checking in C, any word?* and Charli always cringed at that nickname, C, which was from the decade before, when they'd actually considered each other friends. But Charli pretended. That she hadn't heard from me, that she didn't know anything, that my disappearance was as much a mystery to her as it was to my parents. She felt guilty sometimes, but she couldn't say anything to my mom without giving me up, giving all of us up, to LLP and Chrysalis Remington, *Stuck*'s creator.

This time her text read: *Would love to see you if you're ever in New York. Keep me posted, C.* I scrolled up to their previous exchange, where they were talking about Mims and *'90s Mixtape*, which Like-Life Productions had renamed the show after Kipps and I left.

"Why were you asking her about Mims?" I said, sliding the phone back.

"The ratings are falling again." Charli broke up a nub of wasabi with her chopstick, then swirled it in soy sauce. "Which isn't going to be good."

"They don't have a decent heartthrob," Kipps said, then made his face as ugly as humanly possible, scrunching his nose and crossing his eyes.

"You were the real star." Sara pointed at him with her

edamame. "Don't let Jess try to convince you otherwise."

Charli looked at me, then back to her phone, as if she could read my thoughts.

Whenever I heard Mims's name it brought everything back—that day we'd met in her bedroom, which was really *my* bedroom. Watching the scene in Times Square afterward. How Mims ran to my parents . . . how she'd replaced me. I had to remind myself that Mims was only fifteen. Her mom had left her with her aunt and uncle when she was little, and they didn't seem to care much what she was doing. As long as the deposits appeared every week in their bank account, they were happy to continue on as Mims's "managers."

"The storylines are only going to get worse," Charli went on. "The friends she does have will turn on her. Maybe she'll get expelled from school. Maybe Swickley will flood at the end of the season."

"Swickley will flood no matter what." Kipps suddenly seemed gloomy. "Just like the tornado. It's not an enclosed set, and the weather is only getting worse."

"Don't remind us," Sara said under her breath.

I hadn't gotten used to these casual references to apocalyptic doom. After we'd gotten to Maine we'd awoken one morning to dead bees all over the lawn. Sometimes the waves were so rough they'd wash in thousands of starfish, when in the weeks before I hadn't seen a single one. There were tornadoes and hurricanes in other parts of the country, but Sara and Charli had insisted Maine was more temperate. Calm. They weren't afraid of four feet of snow in winter, even though there was nothing about blizzards and hail-storms that felt calm to me.

"You know I'd never tell your parents where you are," Charli went on, ignoring Kipps and Sara. "But if your mom is texting me, the least I can do is try to get information on Mims. Because it's happening again. All the same awful stuff they did to you . . . now they're doing it to Mims."

"Yeah, but what can we do about it? Let's say she wasn't okay, then what?" I asked.

"Just being aware is something. I still feel awful," Charli said, "thinking about how far I let LLP push us. How many times I didn't speak up. I don't want to be that person anymore."

"You're not, though."

"Definitely not," Kipps added.

Charli glanced to Sara, as if waiting for her to respond, but she seemed just as uncomfortable with my questions as Charli, scarfing the last piece of her crab roll in one bite. "I should study."

"It's Friday." I glanced at the clock. "It isn't even eight yet."

"Yeah, but I have a test on Monday."

"What test?"

She hesitated for half a second, then said, "History," in the least convincing way. She gave me an over-the-shoulder hug before slipping down the hall.

Charli tucked the rest of the sushi into the fridge, her fingers pressed to her temple. She and Sara fought sometimes about what had happened inside the set, and I could tell Charli was still sick with guilt over it. Sometimes I'd hear their arguments through Charli's bedroom door, or Sara would inexplicably snap at her. I had to give Charli credit, though; just admitting she'd been wrong was something. My parents still couldn't manage that.

"I can still borrow the car tomorrow?" Kipps asked.

"What's tomorrow?" I helped him grab the last soy sauce dishes off the table.

"I'm getting your super amazing secret belated birthday present."

"I don't need a present."

"You need this one."

"That's tomorrow already?" Charli settled onto one of the stools in the kitchen.

"The car drives itself," Kipps said.

"But there's the location tracker and the GPS. You're going to have to erase all the data as soon as you get there and again when you get back . . . and really, you should delete it and start over a few different times along the way. And then there's the chance that someone might see you on a camera or at a stop light . . ." Charli pressed her fingers to her temple. "This is going to give me a panic attack."

"Sara ordered me a hat and fake glasses."

"I told her not to encourage you. We rarely use the car these days, Kipps." Charli leaned against the sink. "When's the last time you saw us leave the property?"

"But *the present*."

Kipps said it like it was The Present, capital *T* and capital

P, an object that demanded respect. Charli winced at the words, as though it caused her physical pain to even think about it.

"I know, I know." She paused, considering it. "Why don't I go with you?"

"I seriously do not need a present. My birthday was weeks ago," I said. "If it's not safe, it's not safe."

"It's five hours. Six, tops," Kipps said. "We'll leave super early."

Charli let out a long, staggering breath, then went for the keys. Kipps waggled his brows at me, pleased that he'd finally gotten the OK. I wanted to believe him, that it would be fine, that they'd be safe, but there was something in Charli's expression that unsettled me.

"I don't like this . . ." I said.

"It'll be worth it." Kipps held my face in his hands before he kissed me. "I promise."

Kipps left right after the sun came up. He'd slept in my bed, and even at seven in the morning he couldn't keep quiet, banging drawers and stubbing his toe and then fumbling around in the bathroom for a Band-Aid.

By the time he and Charli had gotten out the door I'd forgotten I was supposed to be worried. That leaving the house at all was a risk. Instead I watched them drive off in the SL328, my head foggy, wanting nothing more than to go back to sleep.

I was walking back up the stairs when I noticed Sara's door was open. For our entire lives we'd been less than ten feet apart. In Swickley, before she got fake diagnosed with fake Guignard's Disease, we'd have whole conversations yelling back and forth, until my dad popped his head into the hallway and told us to be quiet. But now I had to go down two flights of stairs and across the living room just to see her. It usually took five minutes before she even opened the door.

"Sar, you up?" I asked, inching closer. It had been an inside joke of ours. Why would you ask someone if they were up, when asking would probably wake them up? It was maybe the most passive-aggressive question ever.

No answer. The curtains were drawn, and the bed was un-made, a pile of throw pillows on the floor. The two projected screens above her desk that were usually on—one streaming the latest episode of *Bolton's Landing*, and another logged in to her Zing account—had disappeared.

Her bedroom in Swickley had been as familiar as my own, but here in Maine everything was different. She was always referencing clothes stores I'd never heard of and mov-ies I'd never watched. There was no candy hidden in her pillowcases or dresser, and this summer she'd confessed she hated it, that anything too sweet made her sick. It had been months and I was still getting to know the real Sara, without the cameras and the constant doctor visits and Charli hover-ing over her, taking her blood pressure or temperature and feeding her pills, all the while pretending they weren't related to each other.

I checked Sara's bathroom, but it was empty. Charli's door was open a crack. The bed was a mess of sheets and blankets, white noise still blasting through the sound system.

The living room and kitchen were quiet. As I padded through the rest of the house I could hear each of my steps on the stone floors. The rooms had the stark, minimalist feel of a museum, white walls with art I pretended to appreciate but secretly hated. Charli was especially excited about a canvas covered in antique keys, but I was pretty sure anyone with access to a garage sale and a hot-glue gun could've made the same thing.

Sara wasn't in my room or Kipps's room, and she wasn't in the front garden or back yard, though there were acres of land I couldn't see from the windows. Charli had installed cameras, partially to watch for any *Stuck* fans on a quest to locate the house, and partially to watch for LLP's security team, in case they ever found out where we were. I went to the utility closet off the kitchen and checked the feeds.

There were ten screens, all trained on different places around the property. One camera was right outside the Illusion Fence and had a clear shot of the beach. It would be weird for Sara to go on a walk, alone, at seven in the morning, but not impossible. I watched and waited. A sailboat went past, but that was it. I almost left to check the backyard again when I caught movement on one of the screens.

The camera was trained on part of the woods, past the vegetable garden Kipps had planted, past a thick patch of trees, but just inside the fencing. It looked like the grass was moving. It drew back, revealing one inch of dirt, then several. The image was in black and white and I couldn't make sense of it, how it was even happening, until three feet of dirt was exposed and I could see the trapdoor. It fell open and then Sara climbed up from a set of underground stairs. She replaced the grass flap over the door and then went to the garden, grabbing a handful of strawberries before heading inside.

I closed the closet and rushed to the back of the house, trying to cut her off before she could get inside. For weeks she'd been disappearing into her room, claiming she had to study or that she was reading, when she'd actually . . . been going to a secret underground bunker in the backyard? To do what? Why was she hiding it from Kipps and me? And why was she lying, after everything she'd done to get me out of the set? When she'd risked so much just to tell me the truth?

She appeared at the edge of the woods, carrying the strawberries in the front of her T-shirt. The bottoms of her flannel pajama pants were wet from the morning dew.

"What were you doing out there?" I asked as soon as she reached the back deck.

"We ran out of strawberries."

"It's barely light out."

"You're up."

"Only because of Kipps. He just left."

Her hair was brushed back in a ponytail and her mascara was smudged beneath her eyes, as if she hadn't washed her face since yesterday morning. She shrugged, then plucked a berry from her T-shirt hammock and held it out to me. I waited, half hoping she'd say it, that she'd just tell me what was going on, but she slipped past me into the kitchen. I stared down at the perfect plump strawberry in between my fingers.

Sara was lying to me. Again.

And this time, I had no idea why.

3

I spent the rest of the morning in my room. Despite having been in Maine for five months, it still felt like a hotel. The sheets were too stiff, the walls too bare. Sara had gotten me a vintage Polaroid camera for my birthday, and I'd hung the pictures down the wall on an emerald-green ribbon. Me and her, me and Kipps, off-kilter selfies and impromptu portraits I'd taken of each of them—scenes from our own three-person universe. My gaze kept drifting to one of Sara and me curled up on the couch. She was laughing at something I'd said, her eyes squeezed closed. You couldn't fake that kind of closeness. At least I didn't think you could.

Kipps and Charli had been gone for an hour, then three, and I didn't want to worry but it was hard not to. Instead I pulled my SmartScreen into my lap and tried to make sense of my latest online physics lesson. Occasionally I'd lean over to the window, watching the backyard, waiting to see if Sara might return to that spot. At some point I fell asleep and woke to her yelling up the stairs. She said my name three times before I finally went to see what she wanted.

"I was calling you. I'm about to eat." She rested one foot on the bottom step. At some point she'd changed into her purple onesie. "Did you want lunch?"

"I'm not hungry."

"Everything okay?" Her voice was casual, light. "They should be back any minute."

"No, it's not that . . ."

She raised her brow, as if to say *what then?* We stood there staring at each other, me on the top step and her on the bottom one, and I kept willing myself to just ask what she was doing outside this morning. But part of me felt like if she lied again, if she even tried to pretend, I'd never forgive her. We were supposed to be past that by now. There weren't supposed to be secrets between us.

One of the speakers beeped and the automated voice announced, "A vehicle is approaching the front gate." It repeated the message in the same lifeless monotone it announced an oncoming hailstorm or a door that had been left open for too long.

"See?" Sara smiled, as if that had solved everything. "I told you they'd be back."

I was halfway down the stairs when I heard the SL328 rip up the gravel driveway, the sound of rocks plinking against the undercarriage. When I got outside Charli was inspecting something on the dashboard. Kipps sat shotgun, and looked more like a sports journalist than a high schooler in the black Lucite frames Sara had found him. He peered out from under a navy Portland Seadogs hat.

When Kipps spotted me across the lawn he tore off the glasses and smiled. "I finally have your very belated birthday present," he called out the window. "I don't know if you will be able to process the awesomeness."

"Try me."

Kipps pushed open the door. A ball of white fur darted across the lawn. As soon as I saw him I knew it was Fuller. I knelt down, pulling him into my lap, pressing my face against his. He was wearing a tiny handmade birthday hat, complete with ribbon and glitter. He was frantic, licking my nose and cheeks and ears, and no matter how much I kissed him and hugged him I couldn't get enough. I'd spent months wondering what happened to him, if he was safe. Did the people who took him know anything about dogs? Did they care enough to feed him and walk him, and did they let him sleep in their room at night so he wouldn't be scared? I tried not to think of the worst scenarios . . . that whoever it was might not be a good person. That Fuller was old. That there was no proof he was even still alive.

Eventually my fingers went to his right ear, looking for the scar from where the neighbor's dog had bitten him. It was there, still a little pink after all this time. He was licking my face and nose so much that it was hard to lift him up, but I managed to find the seven gray, speckled spots across his chest. I counted them twice to be sure.

"It's definitely him," Kipps said. "I checked, like, five times."

"No, I know, I know." I laughed, and that morning and the weirdness with Sara felt so far away. I pressed my head into Fuller's neck, breathing him in. Yeah, he was grimy and hadn't been groomed in months, but the smell always reminded me of home.

How had I lost so much so fast? The house, my bedroom, those winter mornings when I hid under my comforter, not wanting to step out into the cold. In less than a few days, all of it was gone. Playing Connect Four with my dad after we'd set the table and before my mom came in with dinner. Sara running through the woods behind our house, arms outstretched, fingers flicking the leaves, her long braid swinging behind her. The beach at Maple Cove. The old checkered picnic blanket my mom had bought at a garage sale. I remembered the way it looked from underneath, light streaming through, when Sara and I draped it over the piano bench and rocking chair to make our forts.

"I'm so happy you're okay, Fuller." I must've repeated it a dozen times, but I kept my head down, not wanting anyone to see my face.

I hardly registered Sara beside me, scratching Fuller's back. She rested her cheek against him and closed her eyes. "I couldn't believe it either."

"Did I do good?" Kipps roughed up Fuller's fur, making a faux-hawk.

"Where was he?" I asked.

"Sara heard someone had found him," he said. "There was chatter online."

"Kipps was on a mission." Sara's cheek was still on Fuller's back as she spoke. "I got in touch with former extras from the show. And they kept saying that someone had him, that he was safe, but for a long time we didn't know where. Then we heard he was in Massachusetts."

"They'd renamed him *Dog*. I'm sorry, but what kind of monster does that?" Kipps seemed genuinely pissed.

"Who took him?" I asked, as I mentally catalogued what we had in the fridge. He was a glutton for baby carrots and egg yolks.

"I have theories." Kipps pulled his legs around in front of him. "At least, I have theories about who took him from the house initially. The girl he ended up with was this friend of an extra. Analisa. She's just, like, an animal lover who fosters dogs and wanted him to have a good home."

"I don't need theories." Charli surveyed the last inch of the car, then stepped out. "It was Max."

"You don't know that, Mom," Sara shot back.

"Max Pembroke? Our next-door neighbor, Max?"

He was Sara's year in school. In ninth grade he'd had a growth spurt and joined the JV football team. He'd spent every minute before first period making out with Hannah Herlihy, who was at least two feet shorter than him. They used to go at it so hard that you could actually see their tongues jamming together, and they sometimes slunk behind the vending machine so he could feel her up.

"It's been repeated too many times to be a rumor." Charli came toward us, leaning over to adjust Fuller's birthday hat. "It was him and that other kid, his friend."

"Why? Because of all the stuff going on with the extras? The strike?" I asked.

"I suspect it was a bet or a dare," Charli said.

"Who cares why he did it? He did it, and it was messed up. And now we got Fuller back." Kipps pulled the dog into his lap. "The girl didn't even try to bribe us, she was just happy he was going to be with Charli and Sara. She said he seemed depressed."

"Well, you're home now, Fuller," I said, petting the soft spot between Fuller's eyes, which always calmed him. "You're safe."

When I looked up, Kipps was still smiling, a shaggy mess of hair falling in his eyes. I'd given him so much crap for this belated birthday present, which at times I didn't even believe existed. I'd been annoyed he kept dangling it, and skeptical that it could be as good as he'd said it would be, and worried what it meant that he hadn't gotten me more than a promise. It seemed silly now, that I didn't trust him. Because somehow, after everything, he'd been right.

If Sara and Charli hadn't been there I might've side-tackled him, pulled him to the ground and gone all Max and Hannah. The two feet between us felt like its own football field, and I just wanted him close, my arms around his neck, his back. I wanted to tell him I loved him, that it was so clear and sure. Something inside me fired on and I was all need.

I smiled, and it was as if I could see into the future. Every minute unfolding before me, every hour, our noses and foreheads touching as we fell back onto the blanket.

Tonight, I was going to lose my virginity to Kipps Martin.

4

Sneaking out of my parents' house in Swickley was easy compared to this. Everything was timed, and Kipps had to count out loud while we slipped through the first gate at the edge of the property, making sure it wasn't open for more than five seconds, which would alert everyone inside. The Illusion Fence was simpler. The door in the twenty-foot wall didn't have a sensor on it. As soon as we cleared the thin, gauzy screen we were in the middle of the woods, free.

I felt for the key card in my pocket, making sure it was still there. Without it we'd be stuck outside until morning, when Sara or Charli realized we were gone.

"I'm marking it with this branch," Kipps said, dragging a Y-shaped piece of wood through the clearing and dropping it in front of the door we'd just passed through. When I turned back, the house had completely disappeared, blending in with the trees and sky. It was only when I looked closely that I could see the slightest seam near the top of the fence.

"It really is invisible," I said.

Charli had wanted to keep the house as off the map as possible. It wasn't just the superfans who wanted selfies with her and Sara, or a photo of the place to put on their Zing feed. It wasn't just that LLP was still looking for Kipps and me. Some people were furious that Sara and Charli left *Stuck in the '90s*, and others suspected they'd helped me escape. It seemed like every few days some troll was saying something vile about them, or threatening them, and even though Charli and Sara pretended it wasn't a big deal, I could tell it really unsettled them.

We wound through the woods and down the narrow trail to the beach. Sara had told me that there used to be literal beach houses, that people lived right on the water before it became too unpredictable. Now everything was built several stories above sea level, set back a half mile from the coast, where buildings were more protected from storm surges and rogue waves. Charli and Sara's property was on a long, sloping piece of land, to help prevent flooding. It was annoying sometimes, trekking through the woods in the summer heat, but now, just past midnight, it felt like a wonderful secret. We ran, twisting through the trees. When we finally got to the beach it was empty. Thousands of starfish had washed ashore last week but now they were gone, swept back out to sea. Kipps cut in front of me, running, ditching our backpack in the sand. He peeled off his shirt and charged the waves, the water rushing up around his legs.

Some moments are magic, and this one had all the drama of a movie—how the moonlight settled on Kipps's shoulders in blues and golds. His sharp inhale when the waves hit. How he turned to me, smiling, waving for me to join. I had to remind myself no one had orchestrated it, that there was no one behind a monitor somewhere waiting for Kipps to deliver a line that had been written for him. This was *my* life, as I wanted it to be. Kipps and I had created this.

I tossed my dress on the beach and followed him in, the cold water raising the skin on my legs. Kipps had seen me in my underwear before, and out of it, but somehow now I felt more exposed, my nipples visible beneath my thin cotton bra. We swam out to where we couldn't touch the bottom. I felt for Kipps beside me, catching his hands, letting him hold me. The ocean was cold but I didn't feel it, and every time we drifted apart we found each other again. He carried me on his back as each of the waves came for us, trying to take us under.

That first kiss. Wet lips, tasting of salt. Drenched hair clinging to my neck and Kipps pulling me tight against his chest, my legs wrapped around his waist, trying to bring him closer. As soon as we could touch the sand beneath us we started running, the air so much colder now, and as we got out of the water I went for the blanket, fumbling to get it to the ground.

Kipps pulled a towel over us. Behind him, I could see the sky, bright with spattered stars. Droplets came off his hair and ran down his nose. One by one they plinked against my skin and he wiped them away.

"I have a surprise."

"Uh-oh."

"It's a good surprise. I think?"

"You don't sound sure."

He sat back on his heels, and already he felt too far away. Stray droplets raced down his ropey chest. The backpack was on its side, and he rooted around in the dark, eventually pulling out a portable speaker. Charli had given it to us months ago but we'd always just used the house system.

"Romantic music," he said, tapping his phone screen with his finger. "And condoms."

"A winning pair."

A beat, then a few slow and sultry notes. I thought for a second it was a parody song, but then I recognized the first chords of "Lover Lay Down" and started laughing.

"Dave Matthews," he said.

"This is maybe the most nineties thing you've ever done."

"I wanted you to feel at home."

"I am at home."

His hand dropped into mine, and I held it tight. "Too cheesy?" he asked.

"Just cheesy enough."

When he lowered himself on top of me I almost made a request for him to *please, please, lover lay down*, but I stopped myself, trying to hold on to some seriousness, because how can you possibly lose your virginity if you can't stop laughing long enough to even kiss?

"I love you, Kipps."

He swiped a piece of wet hair off my forehead and tucked it behind my ear.

"I love you too." He rested his head against mine, and

our lips were nearly touching, his eyes scanning the lower half of my face. "This is . . . right."

I didn't know words could do that to you. It was somehow better than *I love you*, better than being told how and why. Because that was the truth of the truth, wasn't it? This, what was between us, always felt good and right, even when nothing else did. I arched my neck to meet his lips and then we were together again, and nothing else mattered.

We were a fumbling mess of hands and legs, and I couldn't get my bra and underwear off fast enough. At some point he reached for the condom and I remember the rustle of the wrapper, and trying to help him get it on, and then the heat between my legs. But mostly I remember the way Kipps looked at me, watching my every expression.

5

When I woke up I was still holding Kipps's hand, clutching it to my chest like a rare, precious thing. The music had stopped. Instead his breath was in my ear, his face nestled in my damp hair. The blanket had shifted beneath us and now sand was everywhere—between my fingers and toes, clinging to the inside of my bra, stuck to my cheek. I reached down and brushed the grit out of my belly button.

It wasn't obvious at first. Clouds had rolled in, a fog covering the stars, and it blotted out the light on the beach. They were just shadows moving behind the dunes. *Deer*, I thought. They were as common as mice around here, and you'd see them eating in the high grass or in the woods, a whole herd passing through. But then a flashlight switched on. It flicked across the waves, catching on the whitecaps, and I squeezed Kipps's hand, willing him awake.

He rolled over and pulled me tighter, curling me against his chest.

"Someone's here," I whispered.

His body tensed, and I could feel him behind me, slowly clocking the light that was now just a few yards away. It skimmed across the water. We were tucked behind a sand drift, but it wouldn't be long before they crested the hill. I pulled on my dress.

Kipps fumbled for his bathing suit. He balled up the towel and blanket and threw them in the backpack, along with the speaker. I crouched in the sand, trying to figure out how long we'd been asleep for. Had it had been twenty minutes or two hours? Who the hell would be out here this late, besides us?

"Crap . . ." Kipps pointed to the edge of the shore. His T-shirt sat in a crumpled pile.

"Leave it, it's just a shirt."

"It's my favorite one. Reed gave it to me."

I tugged at his arm, trying to guide him back to the path, but he wouldn't move. It would take twenty minutes to get to the fence, back to the house and upstairs. But as we stood there, debating if he had time to grab it, two men crested the dunes, silhouetted by the moonlit sky. The flashlight beam made one long sweep over the water, then settled between Kipps's shoulder blades.

We ran. The light flicked over us, white-hot against our legs, our arms, our hair. My breath was stuck in my chest. Whoever it was behind us, I heard them sprinting to catch up. The beam was more careless as they ran, shaking, jumping from the dunes to the sand to the water, casting wide, wild arcs and then disappearing into the sky.

Kipps and I scanned the beach, frantically searching for

the path to the house. All the trees looked exactly the same. We were moving so fast and it was so dark, everything blended together. By the time I glanced back the men were already on us. The bigger one yanked Kipps away from me, one hand on his bicep as the other aimed the flashlight at his face.

"Kipps Martin. We thought you might be here."

"Do you know them?" I asked, but already Kipps felt miles away. They'd positioned themselves between us, the bigger one maneuvering Kipps behind his back.

"He does, Jess." The guy was built like a gymnast, short and muscular, his polo stretched over his chest. It wasn't obvious at first, but then I registered the mace and Taser clipped to his belt, the zip ties along his holster. They were the LLP security team, they had to be.

"This is George," Kipps said. He didn't fight. He seemed younger somehow, taking on the slumped posture of a kid who knows they're in trouble. "He works at the Swickley Mall."

"The mall cop?" I had a flash of the man in Claire's, interrogating Kristen about a pair of hoop earrings she'd tucked in her purse as she'd walked out. We'd spent an hour in a basement office, aka shoplifting purgatory, wondering if she was going to get arrested.

The guy just ignored me, instead looping a zip tie around Kipps's wrists. A horrible, empty feeling took hold. LLP had found us here, hundreds of miles from the set.

They'd found Kipps.

"We've been tracking Charli Dean's car for three months now. Weird that some random teenage boy would be sitting in her passenger seat." George kept a tight grip on Kipps's arm as he led him back up the beach.

"You can't just take him," I said, running after them. They didn't even turn around, instead bringing him to where the dunes were higher, a massive bluff overlooking the ocean. When I reached them, Kipps tried to pull away, but they boxed him in. "Where are you going?"

"Where do you think?" the taller one said. As I caught his profile I recognized him as one of the guys from the Swickley Alarms company. He'd played shortstop in my dad's softball league.

"He's seventeen." George was expressionless, his eyes fixed ahead. "Last time I checked, he's not legally emancipated. His parents have been looking for him. End of story."

"Bullshit," I said. "Chrysalis has been looking for him. It's Chrysalis."

They led him across the road, where an SL880 was waiting, its doors spread out like wings. They loaded Kipps into the backseat and I couldn't see him through the tinted windows. The two men climbed in, but before they could shut the doors I grabbed onto the frame of the car.

"Take me with him," I begged. "Take me back."

The shorter one pried my fingers off the frame, then pushed my hands away. When I went to grab hold again, he stood and put one hand on his Taser. The other one he balled into a fist. I had the sudden, terrifying feeling that he might hit me.

"She doesn't want you."

It was an admission without admitting anything.

Chrysalis was behind this, like she was behind everything that had come before. Sara's death and fourteen years of lies and Mims starring in *'90s Mixtape*, as if I'd never existed at all. I tried to get a better view into the car, to see Kipps one last time, but the doors slipped down in front of me, closing him off. Then the car pulled away, ripping down a deserted road.

And just like that, Kipps was gone.

I didn't want to watch '90s *Mixtape*, but I had to. It was the only way I could see Kipps now, even if this episode was especially excruciating. He just sat there, folded in on himself, his parents pacing back and forth in front of the white leather sofa. His eyes were puffy and pink.

"After everything we've been through . . ." His mom was an inch or two taller than his dad, with teased auburn bangs that looked like they'd been shellacked in place. "I'm so disappointed in you, Kipps. We were terrified. I couldn't sleep, not knowing where you were."

"You're seventeen." His dad said it twice as loud as he should have, his hands balled into fists. "Have you lost your mind?"

"I told you I didn't want to be a lead. I'd told you that."

"We each have made our fair share of sacrifices," his dad snapped.

His mom held up a hand, as if that were enough. "What

makes me so sad is that you left your brother here. You're his best friend, and you just left him. You want to lie to us, keep us in the dark? Fine. But you didn't tell him anything about where you were going. What was he supposed to think?"

"You make it sound like Reed's some kind of loner. He doesn't need me," he said. "He has Paul."

Paul Rogers. He'd been an extra in the grade above me. I'd never spoken to him directly, unless you counted the one time he'd asked me to borrow a pencil. Kipps had mentioned Reed was dating him even after Paul left the set, that they'd been long-distance.

"Paul and I broke up three months ago."

Kipps turned, noticing Reed standing in the doorway with his arms crossed over his chest. He looked more like their dad than Kipps did, with chin-length black hair and huge gray eyes.

"What?" Kipps seemed genuinely surprised. "I didn't know."

"Why would you? You weren't here." Reed seemed annoyed, but as quickly as he said it, it passed. "It's . . . whatever. Let's not get into it tonight."

"I really wish you'd turn this off," Sara said from somewhere behind me. At some point she'd come into the room, and now she was leaning over the back of the couch, shaking her head at the screen.

"I can't look away."

"This is exactly what Chrysalis wants. She thinks she can get to you through Kipps."

"Well, she's right." I fell back onto the couch, pulling the throw blanket tight around me. "I feel like someone cut off my arm."

"No one cut off your arm."

I ducked under the blanket, a sickening, empty feeling taking hold. It had been almost a week since Kipps had been taken. We'd tried to find a number to reach him inside the set, an email—anything to confirm he was okay. The more we dug for information the more impossible it seemed. I hated crying but lately it just kept happening. Even Fuller had started avoiding me. Apparently sobbing uncontrollably doesn't exactly read: *I'm the alpha. Obey me.*

"We never should've snuck out," I said. "It was so stupid."

The light filtered through the knitted squares. I could just barely see Sara as she came around the couch and turned off the show. She sat beside me, pulling the blanket down and brushing the mess of hair away from my face.

"It's not your fault . . ."

"How did I go from one of the most romantic nights of my life to this? It's out of a horror movie: have sex, be punished. I guess I should just be grateful I didn't get disemboweled." I covered my face with my hands, remembering how when I'd first turned the show on, Kipps was sitting at a lunch table with Ben Taylor and the rest of the varsity soccer team, staring into space. "They could be threatening him. He's probably terrified. Who knows what's happening behind the scenes?"

"Chrysalis can't do this," Sara said. "We won't let her. You just have to trust me."

I finally met her eyes. "You've got to be kidding."

"What's your problem?" Sara flinched. "I'm not the enemy, Jess. I'm on your side."

I didn't even know how to say it without it being rageful. Four days had passed since I'd seen Sara climbing out of a secret door in the backyard, and she still hadn't explained herself. She'd spent an hour after we'd moved in teaching me how to adjust the settings on the heated toilet seats, yet she'd never mentioned a sketchy underground bunker hidden beneath the grass. I sat up, pushing back the damp hair that stuck to my face. "I saw you the other morning."

She let out a deep breath, and for a second I thought she'd just admit it.

"Saw me what?" she finally said.

"Stop lying to me. You came up those stairs in the backyard. By the garden. I tried to find the door afterward, but the grass all looks the same."

Sara leaned forward, her elbows on her knees. "I was going to tell you eventually."

"Can 'eventually' be now?" I hugged the blanket to my chest. "Because I've heard the whole 'eventually' thing before. And besides, it's pretty awful, Kipps being gone and then feeling like you're hiding stuff from me. That you're lying."

"I'm not lying."

"Strawberries? Really?" I reminded her, and then she started laughing, and I started laughing, because it really was ridiculous, how committed she was to her seven a.m. berry-picking story.

"Okay, okay," she finally said. "Let's make now 'eventually.'"

||||||||||||||||||||||||||||||||||

Of course I couldn't find it on my own. The door was covered with Illusion Grass, which looked and felt exactly like the real thing. It had even withered and browned the same way the lawn had after so many weeks without rain. Sara hit a button on her iPhone and the green material rolled back, exposing the entrance beneath it.

"We like to call it a bonus room . . . other people call it a doomsday bunker." She went down the stone steps first, and I followed, lights blinking on above us. The stairs opened into a basement with a full-sized bed, metal toilet, and sink. The shelves were stocked with glass jugs of water, canned soups and fruits, and various packaged foods. "They design them in a lot of houses now, just in case. Hurricanes, tornadoes, nuclear or biological warfare. I guess it's good to have no matter what, just to be safe. Charli's been uneasy since we left the set. She'd never say it out loud, but I know she's worried one of her trolls might find us here and get through the gates."

Sara went to a small desk in the corner and turned on several screens above it. One showed a livestream of a crowd outside a chain-link fence. Some were holding signs and others were shouting things, though the sound was turned off. The other screen was all text, like a giant news feed or something.

"So . . . you've been hiding out down here?" I leaned in, trying to decipher the second screen.

"Yes and no." She tapped a few keys, and the feed lit up with activity, the posts coming so fast in seconds hers had disappeared to the top. "Welcome to Beyond1998. Three million members and growing every day."

"Beyond1998. A fandom?"

"Whatever the opposite of a fandom is." Sara hit a button to slow down the feed, and I started reading the messages. *Trying to find a lawyer for Kipps*, one said. *No luck. Everyone's afraid LLP will bury them.* Another was about the set: *If anyone has access to the science wing of Swickley High, message me privately. Have a quick assignment I need help with.* "My dad's sister Teresa started it years ago. Partially to keep tabs on me while I was on the show."

Sara rarely talked about her dad, and even now, just hearing her mention him felt like this monumental thing. Charli had been the one to tell me about his accident. Oscar had just gotten his MBA and had been a few months into a lucrative consulting job when a car jumped the curb onto the sidewalk and killed him instantly. Charli had helped put him through business school by waiting tables, and together they'd taken out loans, thinking Charli would have Sara and eventually go back to school to be a nurse. Thinking everything would work out, that everything was just beginning. The debt had been so crushing it seemed like a no-brainer when Charli was approached by the producers through her Instagram page, where she wrote publicly about loss and single motherhood. They told her about a show they were casting. Charli didn't register how messed up it was, lying to Sara for the first several years of her life. She just did it when they asked her to pretend she was our mom's best friend and our nanny. She didn't seem to mind that three strangers were playing Sara's family, or that Chrysalis had whitewashed her daughter, as if Sara wasn't half Mexican. That was still the thing that made Sara angriest about her time on the show—having to act as if Oscar had never existed at all.

"My dad's family never wanted me on *Stuck*," Sara went on. "They were completely against it, which, hey—points for foresight. Wish Charli had had some of that," she said. "My aunt created the feed to give people a space to disagree with what was going on, because it felt like every inch of social media and the fandom sites were devoted to celebrating the show. She kept track of me as she watched each episode, noting if anything seemed off, making sure I was okay. She researched anything that happened with LLP.

"You've met her?" I asked.

"Not in person. Not yet. She lives in Texas. We started FaceTiming after I left Swickley."

"And she's the one who told you about Beyond1998."

"Yeah. I knew I'd be helpful as a former member of the cast. I still feel like I have to undo some of the not-so-great stuff that happened when I was on the show."

"You were a kid, Sar. Same as me."

"But that doesn't change things. When I got out I started hearing all these awful stories from extras and former employees who were mistreated by LLP. Whatever gets likes, whatever gets clicks and views . . . that's what matters to them. They won't let anyone get in the way of their bottom line. It makes me sick, thinking I helped them in any way." She played with the space bar on the keyboard, hitting it until the cursor moved all the way to the right, then deleting it back. "Anyway, this feed . . . it's exploded recently. I write under a random alias, DD9, to protect my identity. There are a few former producers and extras who've come on to help— all under fake names. Ever since the extras went on strike and you escaped, people are turning on the show. They're realizing how wrong it is. More people show up outside the set every day to protest."

I leaned forward, studying the screen with the livestream. I hadn't realized the chain-link fence was the one that sur- rounded the set's cement wall. "There are hundreds of them. I've never seen it like that."

"Yeah, and look at this . . ."

She swiped past the livestream of the crowd, moving to a different view from inside a parking garage. Vintage nineties cars sat beside a few newer models. I thought I recognized Amber's parents' silver Mercedes in the far corner.

"Someone on the cleaning crew placed this camera inside the set. Chrysalis and a few of the high-level producers park here, so we can see when they come and go, who they're with. All extras are supposed to leave the set on the buses, so we can make sure no one is being taken out a different way."

"They don't know they're being watched. That feels like appropriate revenge."

"Kind of perfect, right?" Sara rolled the chair away from her desk, maneuvering it with her heels. "You remember Arthur?"

"Arthur Von Appen. My old guitar teacher, yeah. He tried to tell me about the show. Kipps thought LLP killed him."

"LLP did everything but kill him. They literally ruined his life. They made it impossible for him to get hired outside the set. They drained his bank accounts, had him indicted for wire fraud."

"All because he tried to help me."

"He's in touch with a poster on here, but otherwise he's completely off the grid." Sara rubbed her eyes, and I was suddenly aware of how late it was. It must've been past midnight. "LLP controls everything. They have dozens of venture capitalists backing them. They have contacts in law enforcement. At different DAs' offices. Now there's rumors they have some kind of new product they're developing, something that will completely change the landscape."

"Why would they do that? I thought the *Stuck* franchise was their moneymaker. What would they even gain from that?"

Sara clasped her hands together, then rested them under her chin. She smiled as though she'd been waiting for this very moment, for me to ask her this very question.

"I mean, it's how you keep people buying right? Churn out something new that people don't need and make them think they need it, whatever it is. Everything LLP makes, it's designed to distract and manipulate and exploit. If we're giving them our attention and money and time, then we'll forget that whole states are on fire, that hurricanes are hitting cities every day, that every blizzard is worse than the last. We'll forget that people are unemployed, underpaid, and uninsured. And by the time we remember, it's too late."

"They can't just do whatever they want. There has to be a way to push back," I said.

"We're trying . . . but it feels impossible sometimes." Sara was already typing. She posted about someone named Rae Lockwood, an extra who'd gone missing.

It was how people spoke about LLP that made me feel small. There was always a tinge of resignation, as if it were a fixed situation that could never actually be changed. We could get together online and make sure we had the facts, we could install more cameras to watch Chrysalis and the other producers, but that's all we'd ever be doing—watching. Waiting. Now that they'd taken Kipps and extras were disappearing, it wasn't enough. We had to act.

"What if I went back?"

She stopped typing, then swiveled around in the chair. She squinted as she studied me. "What was even the point, you leaving, if you're just going to go back? What have we even been doing these last six months?"

"What do I need to be in Maine for, to play VR games and take online calculus classes? I'm the perfect double agent. Forget placing a camera, I could spend all day every day inside the set, gathering information for you. Talking to Chrysalis—getting close to her. Getting proof of what they did to Arthur and . . ." I leaned in, reading the name in Sara's last post. "And Rae."

Sara swiveled the chair from side to side, a strand of dark hair falling into her eyes. In her joggers and cropped T-shirt she looked more like she should be playing video games, not plotting to take down one of the biggest media companies in the world.

"The story practically writes itself," I went on. "Maybe I'm having regrets. Maybe I'm missing home. Maybe I'm bitter that they replaced me with Mims."

"The story is rock-solid, yeah. But I don't like the idea of you being in there alone."

"I won't be. Kipps will be there."

"I hate this . . . but I also kind of love it?" Sara's lips twisted into a tight smile, the dimple appearing in her cheek. "The former star of *Stuck in the '90s* helping Beyond1998. People are always posting that we need someone inside the set with real access. A producer or one of your parents. All our contacts are nervous about drawing too much attention to themselves. They'll help out here and there, getting us small things we need, but they're terrified of losing their jobs or being on LLP's radar in any way. But if you went back to the set . . . no one would suspect you. If anything, Chrysalis will just think you're there to be with Kipps."

She leaned back in her chair, looking up at me in a way she hadn't in years. I was the big sister again, full of good ideas. The one who threatened to punch Mark Kaminsky when he wouldn't stop calling her Fart Face on the elementary school bus. When Sara ran for fifth-grade class president, I made all of her posters and fliers and spent the morning papering Swickley Middle School so thoroughly it looked like it had been vandalized. After she was fake diagnosed with fake Guignard's Disease, I slept in her bed every night because she was scared to be alone.

No, there was no point in us hiding out in some underground bunker waiting for LLP to show up one day, or waiting to see what Chrysalis had planned for Kipps this season. It was exhausting, constantly bracing for impact.

I had to go back to the set.

Only this time, it would be on my terms.

7

Charli slowed the car, then pulled to the curb behind the boarded-up gas station. The pumps were covered in black garbage bags, now sun bleached and torn. From where we were parked we could see straight through to the back of the motel. The lot was empty except for an older model JR70 and a sprinter van with solar panels on the roof. A woman with Kool-Aid red hair was hanging wet laundry over the second-floor railing.

"This could be a setup. We don't know this person." Charli didn't turn off the engine.

"He had information that you'd only know if you had worked inside the set." Sara stared out the window. "Maps, casting info. And when we needed a contact to steal a key card, he was the one who made it happen."

Sara had finally told Charli about Beyond1998 this morning before we left. As if having to hide myself in the back footwell wasn't bad enough, that revelation had officially

ruined the hour-and-a-half ride, with Charli alternating between anger (*How could you keep this from me for so long?
You don't think I deserved to know?*) and all her old guilt (*I
should've never agreed to putting you on the show.*). Even
though she'd agreed to help us, she still didn't seem happy
about it.

We sat there, staring across the parking lot at the white
van. Last night we'd spent hours in a private exchange with
someone named Skeletor. It wasn't exactly reassuring, picturing the cloaked, skull-faced villain from He-Man. Sara had
talked to him dozens of times before, and when she floated
the idea of sending an actor back into the set, he asked to
meet in person. He said he had information he couldn't share
with her online. It had taken us forever to get to the motel,
which was off a winding mountain road in New Hampshire,
surrounded by trees in every direction. It was straight out of
a true crime documentary.

Sara pulled out her iPhone, checking an app that scanned
for security cameras in the area and flagged which ones were
in use. It seemed like they were tucked under every awning
or next to every door, those tiny domed eyes staring back at
you wherever you went.

"At least Skeletor's intel was right," Sara finally said,
pointing to the cameras along the back of the motel. "This
is a dead zone. That security system has been down for
months."

"This is creepy." Charli ran her hands over the wheel.
"He can't just tell you this information on the phone?"

"He thinks they're tracing his calls. Besides, if Jess is

going back in, she can't just sit in her room and twiddle her fingers. We need to be strategic. He can help us."

"Yeah," I said. "I'm not a finger twiddler."

Sara was the first one out of the car. Charli and I followed. The sky was overcast, the air heavy with humidity. Even though we were all together it felt impossibly lonely here, dense forest spreading out on all sides, the motel rooms dark. The redheaded woman had already gone inside by the time we reached the van.

We heard faint music as Sara knocked on the passenger window.

The music stopped. A small window in the back popped open.

"We talked over Marketplace?" Sara said, leaning toward the tinted glass. "We're here to pick up the speakers?"

Someone fumbled around inside, opening and closing drawers, and then the door slid back. A plump Asian American woman with wiry gray hair crouched beside it. "Jessica Flynn." She stared at me. "You're DD9?"

"I am," Sara corrected.

"Back from the dead." She looked Sara up and down. "Impressive."

"And I'm the mom," Charli added. "Formerly the nurse."

The woman squinted, not quite able to place her. Charli had let her roots grow out, and she dressed completely differently than she had inside the set—her old wardrobe consisted mostly of pink scrubs. Now she was always in brightly colored joggers or velvet sweatsuits. Her forehead was softer now, more relaxed, tiny crow's feet appearing when she smiled. *She's off the Botox,* Sara had said, and then I immediately borrowed her phone to look up what that was.

"Come in. Have a seat," the woman said, scanning the motel windows.

The van had a large round table in the back surrounded by a banquette, whose silver cushions must've doubled as a bed. I tried not to stare at the woman, who was clad head to toe in purple linen, with a cluster of bracelets on her arm that clinked together as she walked. Every inch of the place was covered with tiny paintings and sculptures. Lilies, roses, and delicate clay orchids were glued to the walls, which were painted the palest lavender.

"Anyone want a beer?" she asked, pulling an amber bottle out of the fridge.

"They're underage." Charli shifted in her seat.

"Right." She cracked the top and took a long, slow sip, then opened a drawer in her kitchen, retrieving an envelope from under her utensil tray.

"Can you fill me in a little bit?" Charli said. "Who are you, exactly?"

"I'd rather not say my real name, if you don't mind."

"Skeletor . . ." Sara started. "For some reason I thought you were a guy. A big, scary guy."

"It's safer that way," she said, sliding in beside me. "If I'm meeting up with someone I don't want them knowing I'm an older woman travelling alone. They might think I'm an easy target. You pick up little habits to protect yourself."

"She worked for *Stuck in the '90s*," Sara explained. "Weren't you a producer?"

"I was one of the editors on seasons nine and ten," she said, between sips of her beer. I couldn't figure out if it was cool or worrisome that she was drinking at noon. "I left right after Sara was diagnosed. That crossed a line for me. It felt unconscionable, putting you through that kind of trauma. But I guess it was all unconscionable, if I'd really been thinking about it. Even back then, they were doing all this stuff to make the show more immersive. To drive audience engagement. Nostalgia as a balm for all the world's problems. Nostalgia as a way to zone out. When everything ahead of you is too terrifying to think about, you start looking back."

"What do you do now?" Charli studied a picture above the woman's head. It was a cluster of wildflowers, painted so realistically it looked like a photograph.

"Whatever I want," she said. "It's lovely."

She dumped the contents of the envelope on the table. A small black box fell out, along with a piece of paper covered in small, neat handwriting. Right beside them was a round silver chip. Our host hit a button on the box and a six-inch hologram appeared, like a tiny, glittering figurine. It was a young woman who couldn't have been more than thirty, with pink hair and a piercing through her right eyebrow. The hologram showed her talking, then smiling, then breaking into laughter. It was only a few seconds, without sound, but it was enough to create a feeling. She was a person you'd want to hang out with.

"Everyone knows about Arthur Von Appen," the woman said. "But they really need to know about Rachel Lockwood. We called her Rae. She was organizing the extras. She's the reason they went on strike. And she's been missing for over six months now."

"She disappeared in February, right?" Sara said, pulling the hologram toward her. "I know people in Beyond1998 think LLP is responsible."

"They most definitely are." The woman took another swig of beer. "She went to work on the twenty-third and her family didn't hear from her after that. The set isn't a black hole. Something happened."

I turned the piece of paper around and read through the notes there. It gave the date she disappeared, with AROUND FOUR PM beside it. Then the words SKYSPACE SUITE.

"What's Skyspace?" I asked.

"It's the name of Chrysalis's suite in Chateau Bleu. We suspect there's a hidden server somewhere in there," she explained.

Chateau Bleu was this over-the-top mansion where Amber had her sweet sixteen (which, I now realized, was probably her twentieth birthday). They always held the junior and senior prom there, and some school dances. I went to a neighbor's wedding and Jessie Finkel's bat mitzvah. I'd never once noticed anything weird, aside from Kevin McManning trying to grind on one of Jessie's sequin-clad backup dancers.

"So you need me to get the footage of what happened in those few hours," I said. "You don't think they've deleted it?"

"I don't. There are thousands of cameras. They're everywhere. Even if most of them were off at that time, I have to imagine at least one was on that day and caught some-thing." Her gaze kept returning to the hologram, to Rae as she smiled. "If I just had some kind of proof that they went after her . . . that they're the reason she disappeared . . . we could take it to the press, to social media. Get people to acknowledge this actually happened. LLP says she quit the show. They keep putting out these saccharine statements about how their 'thoughts and prayers' are with her family, as if they don't know exactly what happened."

"This is a lot to take in." Charli fell back against the seat. "Jess, going back is a huge risk. You don't have to do this."

"I have a level of protection Rae didn't," I said to Charli. "I'll be going back as a lead on the show. If anything happens to me, it'll be very public."

Charli studied the hologram, turning the black box around, as if she were picturing me standing there instead. Reduced down to a three-second animation. A ghost of a ghost.

Her silence was enough to satisfy the woman, who took a deep breath before continuing on. "Once you're inside, we're going to need a way to communicate with you. I have a contact who will arrange that—keep an eye out. She'll give you something that blends in with the set. A beeper, maybe a Magic 8 Ball. You'll be able to message back and forth with Sara. She and I will arrange a drop-off point once you have all the footage uploaded."

Drop-off points, uploads, servers. I tried to keep it all straight, but already I was worried it was too much, that I'd somehow mess it up. The woman must've noticed because she said, "It'll be easier than it sounds. You go in, upload the footage to this chip, then you'll pass it to someone who can get it back to me. We'll walk you through the mechanics of it. Then we'll work on getting you out."

"You've got this," Sara said, sliding the small silver chip toward me.

I pressed it into my palm, wondering how I was going to get so much information onto such a little device. I didn't even have my own iPhone yet, because we hadn't wanted anything in my name that could be tracked. I still borrowed Sara's whenever I needed to look something up.

"I guess we'll be in touch then," I said, meeting the woman's eyes.

"I guess we will."

Then she smiled for the first time all day.

8

I'd only ever been in one parade, when I was twelve. I was
at my most awkward, suspended in that space between
childhood and adolescence, my boobs lopsided and barely
there. My parents had signed me up for color guard through
the local YMCA, even though I showed no talent for flag
spinning, and I looked like an oversized hot dog in the pink
spandex unitard. The Memorial Day parade weaved its way
through Swickley, and we did figure eights, the gold silk
flags rippling in the wind. We'd stopped for one final performance in front of town hall. I was the girl in the back,
tossing and dropping, tossing and dropping, the flag bouncing away from me. I still hadn't figured out what the point
of that particular storyline was for the show (Perseverance?
Acceptance? The Dangers of Joining Marching Band?), but
the memory came back to me now, as I got closer to the set.
Crowds lined the road, ten people deep.

It turned out when you said Jess Flynn, the former star

turned high-profile escapee of *Stuck in the '90s*, was thinking about returning to the show, people actually wanted to talk to you. Charli had gotten in touch with one of her old producers, who'd gotten in touch with Chrysalis, who'd planned this whole publicity extravaganza outside the set. As we got closer, there were even more people waiting for us. Every space in every parking lot was filled. Kids sat on the roofs of cars, or on their mothers' shoulders, their hands shooting up when we drove by.

I smoothed the hair on Fuller's nose, a nervous habit. His chin was resting on my leg, and even though the crowd outside cheered and clapped, he never raised his head. I'd been impressed that he hadn't yacked, considering how far the drive was, and how rarely he'd been in a car. It was easier somehow, focusing on him—how *he* felt, what *he* needed. My insides were knotted up, but it was too late and I was already here. The decision had been made.

The black SL87 had driven itself the whole way from Maine to New York, moving seamlessly around highway traffic and broken pavement, never needing to recharge. As we turned onto a main road I recognized a baseball field, and then the luxury car dealership where Kipps and I had taken (err, *stolen*) the NextGen Cloud. The screen on the front console lit up, and a photo of Charli appeared, as though I'd conjured her myself.

I hit the button to put the call through.

"How are you doing, honey?" she said, staring into the camera. "Almost there?"

"I can practically see the wall of the set." If I put my face against the window the top of it was visible behind the strip mall.

"We're watching it live." She turned and looked at a screen, the light flickering over her face. I heard Sara say something but I couldn't make out what.

"I definitely didn't expect this . . . warm a homecoming."

A row of shirtless teen boys stood behind a metal barricade, each of their chests painted with a different letter. Together they spelled out WELCOME BACK, but it took me a beat to read it, the last guys jumbled into EKCA and a stray B. Considering people's growing skepticism of the show, part of me wondered if they were extras too, if LLP had paid the crowd to show up and make it feel like one big celebration.

"One of the producers called after you left."

"Who? Kristen? Amber?"

"Kristen." Charli's expression grew serious. "She wanted me to remind you of the contract you signed. Twelve months starting today, and then the NDA."

We'd made Charli's lawyer put in a clause about extenuating circumstances, and other impenetrable legal jargon, to try to make sure I wouldn't be sued once I left. He'd argued that my escape in March was caused by emotional distress. I didn't know how we'd spin breaking and entering into Chrysalis's office, and I couldn't exactly run that scenario by him.

"She also seemed concerned there might be issues at the event," Charli went on.

"There won't be," I said, and I meant every word. I'd spent the whole ride practicing. I'd smiled and run through what I might say to Chrysalis or the other LLP producers when I met them, nonsense about it being good to be back, and how grateful I was for the opportunity, and blah blah blah. I just had to fake a level of normalcy until I could get what we needed and get out. I'd never been good at pretending, but I had to at least try.

Sara squeezed into the shot, her cheek against Charli's. "Remember, you're playing the long game."

"That's what I've been telling myself."

I scratched behind Fuller's ear, probably harder than I should've, because he shifted away from me. I couldn't help it, I was freaking freaked out. As soon as I was inside the set, Chrysalis was in charge, and hundreds of cameras would be trained on me, catching even the slightest slip-up. There wasn't room for mistakes, and no matter how much I rehearsed there was nothing that could prepare me for seeing my parents, who I hadn't spoken to for almost six months. The only sentence I'd come up with was *Fuck you*, which probably wasn't the best choice.

"I'm scared." I didn't look at Sara and Charli when I said it.

"Of course you are." Charli's voice was soft. "It would be weird if you weren't."

"Like sick scared," I clarified.

"Pukey?" Sara asked.

"Maybe."

"Try not to get it on your dress." She smiled.

They were both quiet, and then Sara's eyes met mine. I was still surprised by how little we needed to say to each other, that sometimes just a look was enough.

"I guess this is goodbye." I didn't want to hang up.

"It's talk soon," Charli corrected. "You should be able to call us from inside the set."

"I'll try. Talk soon." But I still wasn't ready.

"Soon," Sara repeated. "And good luck."

I reached for the screen, about to hang up, but it was already dark.

The car pulled into a long driveway I didn't recognize. The only time I'd seen the perimeter of the set, aside from on the livestream of the protests, was briefly after Kipps and I had escaped. But this section of the wall looked nothing like the high chain-link fence and stone facade from that day. The car cleared a metal barricade, and I had to roll down the window and scan my finger against a glossy plate to prove I was me. Two members of the LLP security team came out from a booth, checking the trunk of the car before letting me pass through.

There must've been a hundred people, maybe more, mingling on the grass beside the main gate, which had LIKE-LIFE PRODUCTIONS scrawled across it in loopy metal letters. The audience was dressed in bright colors, neon greens and yellows, electric pinks and blues—a sprinkle of human confetti. The small, amoeba-shaped stage floated above the crowd, a sleek white podium on one side. Glass chairs dotted the lawn. As the car pulled up to the entrance the crowd broke apart and people found their seats, leaving only a tall, slim woman and a few men in suits.

Chrysalis Remington. I recognized her immediately from

the broadcast in New York. Thick black liner was smudged all over her gray eyes. She wore a fitted silver dress that read more "nightclub singer" than "executive producer," her ropey arms folded across her chest. If she was happy I was back, she definitely didn't seem like it.

It took me a moment to realize the car had stopped at the edge of the lawn, that I was just sitting there, parked. A few people craned their necks, trying to see if I was coming. I opened the door and let Fuller jump out first. When he reached the grass he sniffed a small circle, squatted, and took a huge shit. I don't know that I ever loved him more.

"You can leave that," Chrysalis said, her lips barely moving. She looked like one of the VR extras from Skyscraper, her face hard and angular. "Welcome home, Jess."

Tiny drone cameras circled me like a swarm of bees. As soon as I reached her she hugged me, and I went all corpse in her arms, rigid and cold. I'd never even met her before, and here she was putting on this display for the audience, for the entire world. I thought of Kipps and Arthur and Rae and just being free of all this, in some imagined future where I was finally on the other side.

"The stage is all yours . . ." she said, and the suits behind her smiled.

Breathe in, breathe out. My lungs felt tight as I stepped onto the platform. When it sensed my full weight it lifted several feet into the air, suspending me above the audience. The podium adjusted to my height, and before I could even think, words projected in front of me on a glassy film through which I viewed the scene. I didn't think I could speak the lines until

I said them, following along as each sentence zipped past.

"Thank you all for the warm welcome." I tried to smile but couldn't. "I'm sure most of you here, and at home, have been wondering what happened to me, the girl you've watched grow up these past fifteen years. I know you have been concerned, just like you would feel about a member of your own family, and I'm grateful to have so many people who care. I feel so lucky."

It was strange, reading this version of me. The cadence was similar to mine, but the sentences were sanitized, scrubbed clean of any personality. Every word felt heavy. Flat.

"Through a series of events that it's best not to get into right now, I began to suspect something was off about my life inside the set. Of course I would end up being right. And of course, like anyone would be, I was furious at my parents and the people around me who had kept this secret from me for years. What I didn't understand at the time was why. Since then . . ."

I'VE SPOKEN TO BOTH MY PARENTS AND CHRYSALIS REM-INGTON, THE BELOVED CREATOR AND EXECUTIVE PRODUCER OF THE SHOW, AND . . .

All lies. I hesitated, unwilling to just let my parents off the hook like this. I didn't want to make them seem like they were better people than they were. For months they'd "checked in" with Charli, but they'd never once publicly apologized or said they had any regrets about bringing me onto *Stuck* as a child. On the talk shows and Instagram Lives they'd done since I'd left, they sometimes made it seem like they'd gotten swept up in the excitement of having their own show, even though the lies had continued for fourteen years. Other times they acted like my reaction was ridiculous, that they were always going to tell me eventually. But they had no problem continuing the show with Mims, eating dinner with her every night, treating her like an adopted daughter. Letting her sleep in my room and wear my clothes.

Sara was right, though. It was a long game.

"Since then I've spoken to both my parents and Chrysalis Remington," I continued, "the beloved creator and executive producer of the show, and I understand why they kept the truth from me. I feel really lucky to have grown up with the *Stuck in the '90s* family. Now that I've had some time to myself, I'm relieved to be back here, safe. My guess is *'90s Mixtape* will be even more dramatic now that I know what's going on."

[SMILE JOKINGLY]

"Because there are a lot of people in my life that owe me an explanation, not just my parents. And I definitely have some things to say to them. But for now, it really is good to be home."

[SMILE WARMLY]

[CONTINUE SMILING WHILE CHRYSALIS COMES ONSTAGE]

I didn't really see anyone's face. The audience functioned as one teeming amorphous blob, people I'd never wanted to talk to or meet. I was vaguely aware of them standing and clapping, and the tiny camera drones circling overhead, zooming out and in, hovering in front of my face like deranged hummingbirds.

Chrysalis grinned as she climbed onstage. She walked

over and put her hand on my back in this gentle, sisterly way, as if we had known each other our whole lives. I had to remind myself that she, at least, had known me.

"It says smile," she said through her teeth.

Startled, I looked out at the crowd and gave them my warmest, *I'm not terrified at all* smile. Then I leaned into her for the photo op, the drones clicking all around us, iPhones emerging from purses and pockets to capture it all.

It felt like it might never end.

9

At some point they escorted Fuller and me into a massive SUV with tinted windows. Chrysalis and I sat across from each other in two buttery leather chairs. The thing drove itself, following a set course as we passed through the main entrance and down a long tunnel. Its walls were lined with neon pink and purple lights, which felt like we'd been launched into a massive pinball machine. She rapped her manicured nails on the center console, a steady beat.

"Season three, episode six," she finally said, peering out from her intense eye makeup. "I think it was technically sometime in October. It was hotter than usual, though, in the eighties and nineties even as we were planning the Halloween episodes."

She was so thin I could see the bones of her sternum. She regarded me like a cat might, and even when she wasn't looking directly at me I knew she was still paying attention, anticipating my every move. Studying me as I smoothed back my hair, as I lifted Fuller so he could look out the window, as I crossed and uncrossed my legs.

"What was season three?" I asked after a long pause.

"You lost your first tooth. Your dad wanted to do that horrible thing where you tie a string to it and slam the door, and you were crying and crying. You were really beside yourself." She leaned forward, the faintest smile on her lips. "I had to step in. Or there was season ten when those actresses we'd hired to play the popular clique got a little out of control with their improvising."

"Elizabeth Haverford?" The blond girl had moved from New York City specifically to torture me. Even at the time, I had felt like she was too perfect a Queen Bee, and now I realized she must've been cast from hundreds, or even thousands, of aspiring teen actresses. "She put tomato sauce on my seat so it would look like I'd gotten my period."

"I took particular pleasure in firing her myself. A real brat, that one." Chrysalis kept her eyes on me. "I care about you, Jess. That's what I'm trying to say."

So she'd hired someone to call me Bubble Butt and play pranks on me . . . but she was also proud that she'd protected me from them? What kind of twisted logic was that?

"You're serious right now?"

"Do I seem like I'm kidding?"

"I don't know what you seem like. I don't even know you."

In an instant her expression shifted, her mouth a hard, flat line. Something about that phrase—*I don't even know you*—had bumped her.

"Well, let me officially introduce myself. Chrysalis Remington." She put her hand over her heart. "I'm the creator and executive producer of *Stuck in the '90s*. I'm the reason your parents have a fat savings fund for your college tuition, and book deals, and partnerships with some of the biggest brands in the world. I'm the reason people in this country have quality entertainment to watch, to lose themselves in, even when the world has gone to shit. I'm the reason sixty-one percent of Earth's population knows your name. Hi."

"I didn't ask for this." I pulled Fuller closer, as if there were a way to lose him, even now.

"Well, here's the thing. I didn't ask to be born in Pensacola, Florida. That's the weird thing about life, sometimes things kind of just . . . happen to you."

The car broke out the other end of the tunnel, suddenly bathed in light. Another security booth sat at the top of the ramp. Chrysalis rolled down the window just enough to show her face and they let us through. We pulled into the back entry of a cavernous garage. It took me a few seconds to realize it was the same one I'd seen on Sara's livestream.

"I'm grateful for all the opportunities," I lied. "Really."

"Good. Gratitude is a good place to start." Chrysalis offered me a tight smile before stepping out of the car. She waved me to follow her into the dented 1995 Toyota Camry beside it. I looked up into the corner of the garage, trying to make eye contact with the camera Beyond1998 had hidden there. I nodded, hoping Sara would see that I'd made it inside, that I was okay. It was the tiniest gesture, but it made me feel connected to her. Safe.

"If you start feeling resentful, just think of your new contract." Chrysalis reversed out of the garage. "Two hundred fifty thousand dollars an episode . . . six episodes a week? How much is that?"

She tilted her head as though she really couldn't do the math. As we pulled around the side of the building, it took me a second to place myself. We were now in the Tower Records parking lot, a line of teenagers wrapped around the side of the building. A few of them had camping chairs, while others sat cross-legged on the sidewalk. Two girls with playing cards were in a heated game of spit.

I'd waited on line for tickets before, once for a concert for No Doubt and another time for the Fugees, and I remember thinking it was weird that either one of those groups would come all the way to Swickley just to perform in Regina Wallace Park. Both times Amber, Kristen, and I had gotten there at the exact time listed on the ticket, and both times the only spots we could find were all the way in the back, the stage partially obscured by massive speakers. This summer Kipps told me the performers had been body doubles and the producers had broadcast concert footage from the '90s on the giant screens beside the stage, the performers choreographing their movements to match.

"It's part of Mims's storyline today," Chrysalis said, buckling her seatbelt. She pinched the metal between her fingers, as if it disgusted her to touch anything inside the car. "She tries to get tickets but can't, and then it sends her on this adventure, and she tries to get this kid to trade his tickets for her old bike."

Mims. There was a slight smile at the corner of her lips when she said the name, and I wasn't sure how to interpret it, if Chrysalis was pleased Mims had replaced me or what. The car zipped down Lark Road. We passed the color streets where Kipps lived—he'd told me his house was on Lavender Court, but there was also Ivory Lane, Periwinkle Place, Saffron Drive, Emerald Terrace.

"Where's Kipps?"

"Right now?"

"Yeah. When will I get to see him?"

"I'll have to check." We stopped at a red light and Chrysalis studied me. "You seem awfully attached to Patrick Kramer, considering you haven't spent much time together . . ."

Charli had told the *Stuck* producers Kipps and I had parted ways soon after we'd left the set, then been helped separately by former extras. I hadn't gotten to Maine until after my eighteenth birthday, after reading an online profile that suggested that's where Sara and Charli were and getting in touch with them through a mutual friend, who we never named, and then Kipps followed shortly after. Charli did her best to make it seem like our reunion was fated, a delightful twist of chance. That she and Sara hadn't hid information for me inside the set. That they hadn't helped us get out.

"What can I say, it was a bonding experience."

"Escaping the set."

"Right."

"Well, then, I hope returning to the set together is equally fulfilling."

We drove past Fernwood Park. There wasn't a single kid

playing on the grass. We passed the Elwood movie theater and a strip mall with Dunkin' Donuts and the Ice Cream Café, which had a toy train inside that circled the perimeter right above the wainscoting. Eventually we turned up the long, winding driveway to Chateau Bleu.

"What are we doing here?" I played dumb as I stared up at the banquet hall. It looked grotesque now, with its Roman pillars and gilded staircase. Even the brick seemed fake, like the kind on a miniature-golf castle.

"I moved my office here a few years ago. I get my best ideas in the topiary garden."

"The topiary garden?"

"Those sculpted bushes. We've got a few lions. An elephant." Chrysalis slid out of the car, and I followed her into the mansion. "A long walk can regulate the nervous system. I find it very soothing."

The air-conditioning felt like a morgue. It seemed too lucky that I'd be in Chrysalis's office so soon, but I followed her past the grand staircase and down a hallway with tacky, gold and vomit-green wallpaper, thinking through what our contact had said. Maybe it was possible to get the footage and leave the set within a few weeks. A month. Maybe I wouldn't be here much longer at all.

Chrysalis pushed into one of the smaller ballrooms. Inside, a curvy woman in pink pleather pants organized a rack of clothes. She smiled when she saw me, revealing adorably crooked teeth.

"Marta, you know Jess. Jess, this is Marta, our head costumer. Did you pull the looks?"

Marta grabbed two outfits, but before she could get a third off the rack Chrysalis clucked her tongue no. "Jess can choose one of those. And tell Rick I want her hair to be season fifteen, but messy. Season fifteen, but a little wild. Like we can actually see the missing five months on her. Oh, Christ, where is he? Why am I talking to you?"

Chrysalis looked to the empty chair and vanity in the corner of the room, then through a set of French doors that led into a rose garden. She didn't see Rick, whoever that was, and that seemed to irritate her even more. She turned to leave, not bothering to look at me when she spoke.

"Come find me once they've fixed you."

10

I studied my reflection in the mirror. Overalls and a baby doll T-shirt with an embroidered sunflower. A hemp necklace sat at the base of my throat. Rick had chopped off all my split ends and styled my hair in two high buns, with long strands framing my face, a dark mocha gloss on my lips. I'd tried to do it this way a dozen times before, but it always looked a little too DIY, the buns sitting lopsided or falling out after a few minutes. I scrunched my nose and stuck out my tongue, pretending to be one of those models in the Delia's catalog.

"What the hell is the matter with you?" Rick was short and stocky, with a white T-shirt that looked like it had been put through a shredder. Whenever he lifted his arms his left nipple slipped out.

"Have you ever seen a Delia's catalog?" I asked.

He stared blankly at me as he zipped a flat iron into its leather case.

"Never mind. It's really cool, thanks."

Rick pointed me to an elevator that led to the penthouse, where Chrysalis's office was. The doors slid open to reveal a desk and seating area. A chiseled twentysomething guy with a man bun sat in front of three screens, scrolling through stills from the show.

"She's waiting for you," he said, gesturing to the suite behind him.

The doors opened to a circular room, the walls and ceiling a powdery baby blue. The floor was glossy white marble. I'd seen upscale 2037 interior design on television, but never in person, and I suddenly had that spinny sensation of being too high up.

"Modern Skyspace was the vision," Chrysalis said. "Petunia Klauss did the redesign a few years ago. Do you know her?"

"I'm still catching up."

"She made a name for herself collecting NFTs. She's since designed the Museum of Social Media in London, the HelioHotel in Dubai. Madonna's master bathroom." Chrysalis perched on the end of a piece of furniture that looked more like a giant mattress than a sofa. She slung one long leg over the other. "Look, Jess. I know you came back to be with Kipps. I never believed Charli's story about you bouncing around between different extras' houses and then just showing up one day, alone, out of the blue. Whatever happened between March and now, I don't really care. You've come back. But there are some rules."

"I'm sure there are." I scanned the room, registering a

seam in the back wall. It wasn't clear if that was the editing bay Skeletor had described or if it was a bathroom, a closet . . . storage. It could've been anything.

"Three hundred and seven dollars," she said, pointing to a sleek globed camera nestled in the corner. She pointed to the glittering screens above her desk. "Five thousand two hundred sixty-five dollars." Then she pinched my overalls. "A hundred seventy-eight dollars. See, even these ten minutes that we're sitting here, in my office, and you're not on camera . . . it's costing us money. Everything inside this set costs money. When someone walks by you, I don't want you to see a neighbor or a sophomore at Swickley High or Mr. Lyle, your study hall teacher. I want you to see a dollar amount. I want you to stop thinking of this town as Swickley, this quaint little place where you grew up, and start thinking of it as a business. You're getting paid now. Keeping viewers happy is your job. Entertaining is a fundamental part of your contract."

"I know the show is about money. I get it."

"No, you don't get it," Chrysalis said. "Because if you did, you never would've left in the first place. Next time the thought of leaving even crosses your mind I want you to picture every person employed on this set. Every extra, every guest star, every assistant and editor and producer. The craft services person. Rick and Marta and everyone in the set design department. Their salaries rely on good ratings. Your parents' jobs rely on good ratings. And everything on this set—"

"Costs money, right," I said, finishing the sentence.

"I've texted one of our producers to come take you to your house to reacquaint you with everything. You're going to sink right back into your old life, under the pretense that you've returned to confront your parents. To find out who you really are. Seeing Kipps come back gave you the courage to own your past, to join *'90s Mixtape*. Viewers are going to want raw conversations. Hard truths. So let it all out."

I could almost see my mom's face, that pained expression she got when I disappointed her. The night I'd snuck out and our house was burglarized, her forehead was lined with worry, and she kept putting her hand over her eyes, as if she couldn't bear to look at me. It felt like a cruel joke, now that I knew it had been a scripted moment. Anything good between us had been tainted by hundreds of lies, Sara's diagnosis and death the worst ones of all.

"We've gotten Kipps's approval rating back up, so we can orchestrate a reunion. We may have to do some interviews to bridge the gaps for viewers, but the romance between you and him has always been baked into this last year of high school. Falling for Kipps is one of the only good ideas you've had these last few months."

It wasn't an idea, or a plan, but I couldn't explain that to Chrysalis. It was clear she thought everything, even love, was some kind of manipulation.

"What about Mims?" I asked.

"Mims is done."

"Done?"

"Fired. Her aunt and uncle have been giving us all sorts of problems anyway, and then the ratings . . . oof."

I didn't even like Mims, but I still felt sorry for her. You only had to watch five minutes of *'90s Mixtape* to realize she was thrilled to be on it. She seemed weirdly ecstatic, even in scenes where she shouldn't have been, like when she failed a pop quiz on *Macbeth* or when Ben Taylor threw a snow cone at her head. I didn't even watch the show and I'd seen the clips on social media.

Chrysalis stood and let out a long, dramatic sigh. "Jess, it might be hard to believe but I have a lot of love for you. I want this to work. But it's going to take both of us."

"It's going to work. I want to be here, Chrysalis."

It was weird, how believable I sounded. It wasn't a lie, though. It was going to work because it had to work. Now that I was inside the set, my only way out was with Sara's and Beyond1998's help.

"I like that." Chrysalis leveled a manicured finger at me. "You go. I'll be in touch soon."

Chrysalis sat back behind her desk, several screens between us now, a shimmering veil. She swiped through footage from inside the set, then pulled up her email and started typing away as if I'd completely disappeared. I stood, taking in the room one last time. One wall had an abstract painting of a half-naked woman who looked disturbingly similar to Chrysalis. It was big enough that there could've been a door behind it. It was at least a possibility.

Before I reached the exit Amber pushed inside. She stood there, her purse slung over her shoulder, staring at me like we'd never met before.

"Amber's the producer you texted? She's the one taking

me to my house?" I don't know who I was expecting, but this felt particularly malicious. Amber—or Kiki Wilder—had spent six years pretending to be my best friend, when in actuality she was a twenty-year-old influencer with 18.6 million followers and the host of the latest *TRL* reboot. "Can't someone else do it?"

"Ouch," Amber said.

But Chrysalis ignored me. Amber and I just stood there, staring at each other.

It felt like years since we'd been friends.

11

Amber's mom's Mercedes. The silver convertible had been its own character on the show, a mythic beast that taunted us from the garage, its top folded down, perpetually gleaming from a fresh wash and wax. When her parents weren't home we'd sometimes hang out in it, pretending Amber was driving us, though she never dared touch the keys. Now I was sitting shotgun, stopped at a red light. My arm was slung over the door, my hair whipping around in the wind, and it was exactly as cool as we'd always pictured it would be. I might've said that to Amber, had I not been so ripping pissed at her.

"So that Exxon station." Amber pointed across the intersection. "If you go into the bathroom, there's a stall that—"

"Is out of order, I know," I said. "And if you go through it you can get into Mr. Rutherford's backyard, and his house is actually tech support. You can get a new mic battery or a camera placed or whatever."

Kipps had told me about the passageway that day we'd left the set. There was something particularly annoying about hearing it again, from Amber, who'd once used it right in front of me and then lied about it.

"Oh. I didn't realize you knew that."

"I heard about it after I left."

"Right." She paused, the sound of the blinker filling the silence. "If you're ever hungry, you can go through the whole routine of buying food—from the cafeteria, a restaurant, wherever. But then there's a ton of craft services spots across the set. There's one in the back of the 7-Eleven, behind the Slurpee machine, and another in the post office on River Road. A lot of students use the one right by the cafeteria, because the food is a hundred times better. I'll have to show it to you this week."

"I'll figure it out."

"It's not obvious."

"Whatever."

Fuller was curled up beside my feet, and he'd occasionally glance from me to Amber, as if he were trying to make sense of us. They say dogs can feel tension, blah blah blah, but right then it seemed true.

"So this is your car," I said. "This was always your car."

"Kind of. Not really." She turned right onto my street, a little too fast, and Fuller slid across the foot well. "My parents, my sister, and I . . . we all use it sometimes, if we need to get around inside the set."

"So you've driven it before."

She didn't say anything, and I didn't say anything, because

we were both thinking about those afternoons in the garage and how Kristen had once accidentally spilled her Coke in the back, and we'd all rushed around, mopping the leather seats.

"I meant to say . . . the Willow Creek Mall. It serves as wardrobe for the entire set, the extras, everyone. Anything you see there, it's yours. Most of your outfits will be curated by Marta, and Helene likes to be part of that process as well. But if you really love something, go for it."

It was weird, the way Amber said my mom's name. Helene, one word. Like Rihanna or Kanye. I didn't care who she was inside the set, or how much power she wielded, the days of her treating me like her doll were long over. It was infuriating too, thinking of how I'd scraped together thirty-seven dollars in babysitting money to buy my favorite striped dress from Contempo Casuals. Like . . . WTF? Where had that money gone?

"Here we are." Amber put the car in park in front of my house. The driveway was empty. Someone had left the hose running under the maple tree, and a river raged along the curb.

I let Fuller out as Amber went around back, grabbing a seafoam-green Caboodle case out of the trunk. She balanced it in one hand and held the keys in the other as I followed her up the front steps. Fuller rushed forward before I could stop him, disappearing into the kitchen. I half expected imposter Fuller to attack him, but a minute passed and I didn't hear anything. The house was empty. "That dog is gone?"

"Figured the real Fuller was better."

"You didn't . . ."

"No, we didn't kill him. I'm not a psycho, Jess."

"It's not a ridiculous question. Considering."

Amber ignored me, dropping the Caboodle near the door. Everything felt different now, false. I'd seen our living room set and dining table branded on Nostalgia Bomb, an online furniture store. The glass blocks that lined the foyer looked horribly out of style. My mother had begged Sara and me to do a family photo at Sears the fake year before Sara had fake died, and it was still proudly displayed above our piano. My dad had his arm slung around my mom and they looked happy, in love, even though they'd given an interview titled "A Marriage in Crisis" that very month. Even Sara wasn't Sara. The makeup department had put gray shadow under her eyes and contoured her cheeks so they looked sunken in.

Fuller nosed his bowl in the kitchen, looking for food. "I think I can take it from here," I said as I flicked the light on. I opened the bottom cabinet where the dog food was, took one heaping scoopful and dumped it into Fuller's bowl.

"Just a few last things," she said. "Almost everywhere in the house has cameras, except the bathrooms and few dead spots like this . . ."

She slipped past me and into the pantry. She felt along the top shelf and then grabbed a can of tomato soup in the back and moved it a full foot to the right. Within seconds, the far wall slid back, revealing a room with a couch and desk. There was a virtual window, a giant framed screen that projected an image of a forest with snowy mountains in the distance.

"It's your mom's office."

A light blinked on as I stepped inside. Copies of my mom's latest book, *Overcoming Obstacles*, lined the shelf, along with a tabbed copy of her '90s interior design book and a stack of autographed photos. They were all the same picture—her in a pair of biker shorts and an oversized sweatshirt, chin resting in her hand.

"See? Worth having me here for an extra five minutes, right?" Amber said, pulling her braids down over one shoulder. "Want to see more?"

I didn't respond, just followed her through the house. Down in the basement, she showed me how to move the hot-water heater to access a door behind it. It connected with a tunnel that led to our next-door neighbor's garage. Inside was a lounge with a minibar, a bathroom, and additional outfits supplied by the wardrobe department. She pointed out the cameras behind the mirrors in our dining room and hallway, and then showed me my dad's office, which was hidden behind the giant wood desk in our den. You had to crouch down to get inside.

There were cameras in ceiling fans and perfume bottles. The hideous glass sculpture in my parents' bedroom had two cameras in it, and there was another in their VCR. Charli's lawyer had negotiated for me to have control over the ones in my room, and Amber showed me how to use the mute button on my television remote to switch them off whenever I wanted.

"Lucky me," I said, an edge in my voice. "I get a few measly seconds of privacy."

Amber had just reached the bottom of the stairs. She

stepped into the living room, then turned and glared up at me. I still had the remote control in my hand. "You're the one who wanted to come back to the show. No one begged you to be on '90s Mixtape. You can't be pissed at me and also expect things to magically go back to normal."

"If my life six months ago was normal . . . then yeah, things will be different this time around. And I'm sorry if I don't actually trust anything you say, but I don't."

"This is my job." Amber said the words slowly, as if they were hard for me to understand. "I started on the show when I was fifteen, Jess."

"You pretended to be my friend."

"I wasn't pretending."

"Right."

She parted her lips, as if she might say something else, but then decided not to. Instead she grabbed the Caboodle and dug through it. She passed me the iPhone inside. "This is yours. Kipps's phone number is already in the contacts. Chrysalis would prefer you not to use it on camera, but with '90s Mixtape anything goes. The audience knows that Mims came on as your replacement and is more like a pseudo-daughter to Helene and Carter. Everyone saw your escape and knows that you're in on it now, and that you know it's not September 1998. So say whatever you want to your parents . . . or maybe not *whatever* you want. But you can be honest. The audience is expecting a lot of drama, even if that means breaking the fourth wall."

I scrolled through the phone's contacts. She was right, Kipps was there. Chrysalis and Amber too, along with

Chrysalis's assistant, who didn't seem to have a name beyond CHRYSALIS ASST. Before I could say anything Amber pointed to a few pieces of jewelry in the Caboodle. A mood ring, a Joe Boxer smiley face watch, a hemp necklace with a glass bead in the center. I recognized a pair of enamel daisy earrings from Claire's. "These have mics in them," she said. "You're going to want to have at least one on at all times. Try not to take them off, even on breaks."

She was still sitting there, rooting around in the bottom of the thing, and I just wanted it to end. We could do this for hours, her showing me secret passages inside the house, or pointing out cameras, or explaining the most recent storylines of the spin-off show. It wouldn't change anything or make anything better. Too much had already happened between us.

"I got you this," she said, handing me a bag. It took me a second to realize it wasn't just a bag, it was *my* bag—the one I'd given to Mims five months before. It still had everything inside. My Keroppi change purse, with a handful of quarters and dimes. My wallet, complete with my learner's permit and Blockbuster card and a punch card from Gino's Pizza. There was my old Lilith Fair ticket stub, and a friendship bracelet Kristen had made me, which seemed pathetic now next to the paper football note with my name on the front, printed in Tyler's block handwriting. They were strange artifacts from another life.

"How'd you do that? Isn't this . . . Mims's now?"

"It was always yours. You got it at that arts fair on Apple Street. Sophomore year?"

I'd completely forgotten about it. The woman selling them had embroidered the tiny flowers onto the canvas herself, and she'd taken a dollar off the price because my mom had designed her kitchen. Amber was still looking at me, waiting for a reaction, and I knew I should thank her. She'd remembered where I'd gotten it, and that I'd loved it, and she'd gone out of her way to return it to me. I was supposed to be polite. This was supposed to mean something, but I could feel every camera on me now, watching, waiting. So I dug through the bottom of the bag and retrieved the friendship bracelet, holding it between us.

"Would you give this back to Kristen?" I asked. "I don't want it anymore."

Amber's smile disappeared, and for half a second she looked like I'd slapped her, her expression a mix of hurt and shock. It took a beat before she steadied herself, then let out a small, awkward laugh. She took the bracelet and shoved it into the back pocket of her jeans. When she smiled it was convincing, and I was just a little bit jealous then.

She'd always been a great actress.

12

The Goldilocks fairy tale had taken on new meaning. Walking around in the dark, empty house—*my* dark, empty house—I heard those lines everywhere. *Someone's been sitting in my chair*, I thought when I found Jolly Rancher wrappers wedged between the couch cushions. *Someone's been eating my porridge*, when I noticed the half-empty Snapple pink lemonade in the fridge. It was creepy, the way everything was just a little off.

When I turned on the light in my bedroom it was like staring at one of those WHAT'S WRONG WITH THIS PICTURE?! activities in the back of *Highlights* magazine. There were balled-up tissues covered with lip gloss sitting just inches from the trash can. My brush looked like a hamster had died on it, a fat wad of brown hair clinging to the bristles. Mims had lined up my perfume bottles in a row as if they were action figures, and GAP Dream was nearly empty, even though I'd bought a new one the week before I'd left. It was all too

weird and off-putting to deal with, so I dropped the Caboodle and my purse and beelined for the tree house, hoping at
least one spot had remained untouched.

Outside, the cool air was a relief. I climbed the boards
two at a time, skipping the broken one in the middle, and
hoisted myself up onto the platform. I combed every inch of
the walls and floor, tossing anything that looked like it could
be a camera: the wooden crate we used as a table, a matted
Popple Sara had refused to get rid of, some crusty bottles of
Hard Candy nail polish. I threw it all out the window, satisfied as it hit the dirt.

I checked and double-checked the lantern before deciding
it could stay, but tossed Tyler's hoodie, a relic he must've left
back in March. It was hard to be here and not to think of
him . . . of us. My head on his chest as we watched *Dazed
and Confused* for the fifth time. How he'd brought his whole
stereo one afternoon just so he could play me this cassette
he'd bought, a new band called Weezer. Me telling him about
Sara, and her diagnosis, and his hand on my shoulder as I
tried not to cry, and then cried anyway, because what were
friends even for?

What. The. Actual. Fuck.

Looking at the wood shutters Tyler had nailed himself, the
carved TS + JF above the door, I told myself the same thing
I'd told myself a hundred times over the past five months:
There is no Tyler Scruggs. Tyler Scruggs does not exist. No
Fire Crotch, no Bugsy Scruggsy. There is no one to love and
no one to miss. There is only Roddy Perkins.

Roddy Perkins, who still did interviews, almost six

months later, even though he'd said everything he had to say within the first two weeks of me leaving. Roddy, who was most definitely behind the spate of personal items being auctioned on eBay—including the grilled cheese sandwich (with plate!) from the day I'd left. I leaned back on the musty pillows and stared at the ceiling, trying to figure out how I could change the TS + JF to something that didn't make my skin crawl. A star? Could I carve the TS into an SF?

I'd never had an iPhone before, so I'd forgotten it was in my back pocket until I felt it there, a glass block against my hip. I scrolled through my whopping four contacts, and just looking at Kipps's number was enough to bring me back to myself. For the first time since we'd met, I had Kipps's phone number. That somehow made everything feel more legitimate, and it was hard not to imagine being curled up in bed, talking to him after everyone had gone to sleep. I dialed and listened to each ring, the silence between them unbearable. Then, his voice.

"This is Kipps. Leave a message."

Sara had warned me voicemail was a trap, so I just hung up. You should never leave a message for anyone, ever. She was the one who'd taught me how to text, all that BRB and MOS and RN stuff, and then she'd gone on this whole rambling tirade about people who call and then expect you to call them back.

I pulled up a new text to Kipps.

THIS IS NOT THE REAL WORLD

4:38 PM

It's me, Jess. Did you see the press conference?

Jess Flynn????

No, the other Jess!

Thompson?? Weinberg???

FLYNN!! I'm going to murder you.

it really is u
how r u texting?
is this Sara's phone?
wya?

wya???

where r u?

I'm inside the set. LLP gave me an iphone.

whoa
why did u come back???

Call me.

95

I can't

my parents are yelling

I'm at my house.

this is bad

I promise it's good. Trust me.

Wait, so you didn't see the press conference?

def not . . . I'm on lockdown over here. its tense

WHY DID U COME BACK???

For you.

It was weird to see it like that, in writing. Maybe that wasn't the whole truth, or even half, but it was the only truth I could admit to right now.

love u

will call asap

Maybe we'd already said too much. But all I had wanted for the last few days was to talk to him. I needed that closeness. I needed *us*.

LYT.

Maybe it wasn't a real abbreviation. I didn't know, but I typed it anyway. I watched the screen, waiting for that ellipsis to appear, but that was it. He'd left. The screen blinked off and my eyes adjusted to the dark.

It couldn't have been more than a few minutes that passed, but I understood it now, the loneliness that crept in when you had too much time and space to think. I had the weird impulse to pull up a stupid game like Kitten Smash or CannonBall Run just so I didn't have to be alone with myself. I kept seeing Kipps being dragged across the dunes, how small and scared he seemed when he glanced back, looking at me one last time. What would have happened if he never went to get Fuller? Was it possible LLP never would've found us? That we'd all still be safe, back in Maine?

I went back to my iPhone and typed the only number I knew by heart.

13

Sara picked up on the first ring.

"I told you not to call people. It's aggressive."

"You just called me the other day."

"No . . . Charli called you." Outside the sun had almost completely disappeared, the last bits of light dancing across the wall. "Which kind of proves my point."

"Whatever. I'm in the tree house."

"Throwback . . ."

"Weird, right?"

"Beyond." I could hear Charli's voice in the background, then Sara shushing her. "Charli says hi. We watched the press conference."

"What'd you think?"

"I mean . . . Fuller looked very handsome. I forgot how telegenic he is."

"That bad?"

"It's just . . . I could tell what you were thinking. Every

minute of it."

I instinctively reached for the phone cord, forgetting it wasn't there.

"Chrysalis had Amber take me back to the house. Amber."

"That's awkward."

"She gave me an iPhone to use. Or Like-Life Productions did, I guess."

"The one you're on?"

"Yeah."

Sara was silent, and I knew exactly what that meant. I immediately revisited everything I'd texted to Kipps, wondering if it was stupid to just blurt that all out. Maybe I didn't tell him much, but I'd told him I loved him, and that was enough to feel exposed. I didn't need Chrysalis knowing about the intricacies of our relationship, then using them to manipulate me.

"Jess—just be careful."

"I know."

I stared at the *Bop* poster on the tree house wall, the paper worn and discolored at the edges. Sara was the one who'd been obsessed with Andrew Keegan. I'd let her put the centerfold up right after her diagnosis, even though it was a little embarrassing how he stared down at Tyler and me every time we hung out, the strangest third wheel.

"You there?" Sara's voice on the other end of the line.

"I'm just making eyes with Andrew."

"Tell him I miss him."

"I will. He—"

The light on the wall changed, a perfect gleaming square

appearing out of the dark. I sat up and looked out the window.

"Jess? You're scaring me."

The lights in the kitchen were on. Someone was home.

"Don't be scared."

I wasn't trying to be brave. Any nerves from the day had left me, replaced instead by a sudden protectiveness. For Sara, and maybe for myself too. As I watched my mom set her purse down on the kitchen counter, something surged inside me.

"I have to go," I said. "Mom is home. I mean, Helene."

"Yikes."

"Love you."

When I got to the house, I threw open the kitchen door and the lights hit me, bright and blinding. My mom looked genuinely surprised, her hand coming up to cover her mouth, her other hand clutching her chest. I could've sworn she wasn't faking it, but it was impossible to be certain. It was impossible to be certain of anything anymore.

"Oh my god, Jess. You're here. You're home." Her voice was unsteady, and when she threw her arms around me, I let her. I could feel her choked breaths, her hand coming up to wipe her eyes, all the while trying to hold on to me. "I can't believe you're home."

I let my arms rest on her back, and it was the tightness that got me, how she locked me there and didn't let go. I didn't want to feel anything, not now, not on camera, but a fire rose behind my eyes. The good memories came back, the comfort. Her hand feeling my forehead when I was sick or the elaborate cakes she'd make on my birthday—ones I'd actually seen her decorate herself in a late-night frenzy, the kitchen a mess of colored frosting. I didn't want to feel anything, but how could I not? How could I not feel everything, coming home?

There were footsteps on the stairs, then my dad was there, his big arms wrapped around us both. "When? How?" He closed his eyes as if he were savoring the moment.

"I got back this afternoon."

When I pulled away their faces were pink and wet. My mom brushed back her wispy blond bangs, trying to fix herself, and I turned, noticing the camera in the microwave. She grabbed a paper towel and pressed it to her cheeks. "I just can't believe you're here. I was terrified. I didn't know if you . . . I didn't know what happened. It can be dangerous outside the set. And those videos you left . . ."

My dad rested one hand on the counter, starting the interrogation.

"Where were you?" he finally said.

"*Where was I?*" I repeated.

"You left and didn't say anything." He straightened, crossing his arms over his chest.

"What was there to say?"

"Okay, let's calm down." My mom held up her hands, and her eyes darted again to the camera in the microwave. At some point she'd tucked her hair behind one ear and sat down in a chair, giving herself a better angle.

"Don't worry, you look great. Really."

"Excuse me?"

"The camera in the microwave." I moved toward it, my

nose just inches from the buttons and the glassy panel above them, where everything was hidden. "Really, that's a great angle for you. Did you want to take a minute to fix your hair, Dad? *Carter?*"

"Do not speak to me that way." He tried to sound stern but seconds later his hand went to his hair, combing a thinning patch at the crown as though I'd triggered some deep insecurity.

"Jess, we were always going to tell you. We were just waiting for the right time." My mom smoothed the table with her hand. "It just felt like a lot to take in."

"You know what felt like a lot? Sara getting sick. Sara dying. That felt like a lot for me to take in. It's . . . you're messed up. This is all so messed up, you know that?"

"Then why did you come back?" My mom looked stunned. "If it's so terrible here, if we're so horrible, why did you come back?"

To get information for Beyond1998. To be with Kipps. To do something, anything, besides wait. I couldn't just say that, though, so instead I let the silence swell between us.

"You came back because it's pretty good in here. You had everything you ever wanted. It was a good life. You've seen what else is out there now. This is a great life we've made for you, and you know it." Her voice was so strained as she said it, I almost felt sorry for her. "Admit that we did some things right."

"Sara and Charli wanted to leave the show. That was their choice." My dad was still fiddling with his hair, tousling it at the roots. "They agreed to that storyline as an exit. Chrysalis wanted something dramatic, something real."

"None of this is real. None of it."

My mom rested her head in her hands, as if it were a great inconvenience, me being here saying what I was saying. I didn't know how I'd become the villain of this story, the enemy. She didn't want to hear about how it made me feel to watch Sara get sicker and sicker. She didn't want to know how it had hurt me.

I should've stopped there. Maybe. Probably. I should've known better than to keep arguing, but part of me was sure that if I could just explain it a little better, a little more clearly, then they would understand. I needed them to understand.

"I never agreed to this. To any of it," I said. "I was on camera all the time. I mean, all these private moments. All of it was on camera. My first kiss, my first bra . . . changing in the Macy's dressing room—"

"That wasn't on camera," my mom cut me off.

"I saw those stupid mugs with my seventh-grade picture on them. And how you let people vote on my outfits and on whether I should play the guitar, and how you kept insisting I cut my hair a certain way and wear this kind of lip gloss and it was all—"

"Enough!" I'd rarely heard my dad yell like that, his voice booming through the kitchen.

"I didn't realize I was such an awful, awful mother."

When my mom looked up, she was crying. She grabbed one hand with the other, and I noticed they were shaking.

She was trying to steady herself. I'd never seen her like that, but maybe it was because I'd never actually *seen* her. It was impossible to know where Helene Hart ended and Joanna Flynn began.

"I'm sorry, I didn't—"

Before I could say anything else she got up and went to the bathroom, the door banging shut behind her. There was something about her rage that felt honest, true, as if I'd pulled back the curtain, revealing all the messy parts of us.

"Are you happy now?" my dad asked. Then he turned out of the room, following her. I heard him knock on the door. His voice was gentle, almost a whisper. "Helene? Helene, it's me."

So this was Helene Hart.

This was Carter Boon.

No more Sam Flynn, no more Joanna Flynn. These people were my parents, behind the fake smiles and teased bangs and neon nineties windbreakers. Without the curated Instagram feed and the book deals and the branded protein shakes. They were angry and untethered and even a little petty, and maybe I was too. I'd never had the chance to say what I wanted when I wanted, or to even know the truth. It felt like the beginning of everything, of us being who we really were.

I turned back to the camera on the microwave. The small, tinted glass window was just transparent enough that I could see through it. The bulging eye of the camera stared at me. *Are you happy now, are you happy now?* Those words repeated in my head, and I let out a long, slow breath, feeling a rush of relief.

Yeah, maybe I was.

14

I had to walk past the bathroom on my way up the stairs. At some point my mom had let my dad inside, and I could hear their muffled voices behind the door. They didn't want to be on camera. They didn't want anyone to see them like this—crying, wounded, vulnerable. They wanted their private moments to be private. I could almost hear Alanis Morissette's voice in my head. *Isn't it ironic? Yeah, I really do think.*

After everything that had happened, all I wanted was the weight of my comforter, the warmth of my bed. But as I made my way down the hall, I knew it wasn't that simple. Not anymore. It didn't matter if Chrysalis had fired Mims, she'd already worn every piece of clothing in my closet. All my magazines had disappeared, and the picture frames on my dresser had been rearranged, some taped over with photos of her and Kristen or her and Amber. She'd shoved my guitar under my bed and instead put an inflatable chair in that corner, even though it looked cheesy, the neon pink clashing with everything else in the room. I'd have to wash my clothes and sheets twice to get rid of the unfamiliar smell.

When I flicked my light switch nothing happened. The bulb must've been out. I moved to my desk, tripping over a pair of Steve Madden slides, until I found the lamp. As soon as I turned it on I heard her voice, as clear as it had been that day in her apartment.

"Hey . . ." Mims was lying on the bed, headphones covering her ears. She tugged them down around her neck. "Jess?"

"Mims?" I could barely get the word out. "What are you doing here?"

"What am *I* doing here? What are *you* doing here?"

She sat up, her face half in shadow. It didn't matter how many times I'd tried to avoid watching, I'd still seen clips of the show—five minutes here, another five there. I could tell something was different about her, but it was only seeing her here, in person, that I realized what it was. When we'd first met her she'd had a gap between her front teeth, but now it was gone. Her hair had golden highlights in the front and her skin had that dewy, serum glow I'd seen in dozens of Zing ads. She wasn't just a sixteen-year-old girl anymore, she was a television personality. Someone plucked and primped for the cameras.

"I'm coming back to the show . . ." I reached for the iPhone, wondering if I was supposed to call Chrysalis. She'd said Mims was fired, done. Did she know she was still here?

"That's weird." Mims's mouth twisted to the side.

"Well, technically this is my house. Those people downstairs are my parents."

"So what?" She rolled onto her side. "I'm supposed to sleep in Sara's room now? That's creepy."

"No, um . . . I think . . ."

I was suddenly hyperaware of the camera in the ceiling fan. This wasn't an accident. Of course it wasn't. Chrysalis had left this to me. I was the one who'd fire Mims, who'd deliver the news, on television, for everyone to see. As much as I hated playing along with her game, part of me was still furious with Mims, and it seemed like Chrysalis somehow knew that and was leveraging it against me. Mims had lied to Kipps and me, took the information we'd given her and used it to win herself a spot on the show. I had sympathy for her, I did, but she was a shameless opportunist.

I searched the room for the remote, hoping I could just shut the cameras off, but it had disappeared from its perch above the television. That didn't feel like a coincidence.

"Look, Mims . . ." I tried. "Chrysalis said you're leaving the show. That you have to go home."

Mims rolled her eyes. "Sure, okay, Jess."

"I'm serious."

"So they're just like . . . letting you back? After everything you did?"

Her Discman was still on, and I could hear Counting Crows drifting out of the headphones. "Mr. Jones" ended and "Perfect Blue Buildings" began.

"This is my room. You are literally in my room right now," I said.

"So what?"

"So you were never supposed to be here in the first place.

Don't you remember our deal? You went rogue. You decided not to post that second video."

Mims looked past me to my bookshelf. I couldn't remember which perfume bottle the camera was hidden in, just that Amber mentioned one was there. "I didn't post it because I didn't want to hurt your fans. I actually care about the fans, Jess. I care about the fans because I was one."

"Right . . ."

"You should've seen it." Mims was so focused on the camera now, it was like I wasn't even there. "She wanted to tell all of you how you'd used her all these years, how you'd watched the show without her permission and she didn't belong to you. She doesn't care about the *Stuck* family at all. I've tried to warn you—she only cares about herself."

I moved into the corner of the room, finding my desk chair and sliding as far back as I could, trying to get space from her. In some ways, she wasn't wrong. But this wasn't about me anymore. This was Mims's monologue, her last great performance before she left. The final five seconds of her fifteen minutes of fame.

"I was the one who kept the show going," Mims went on. "I'd watched *Stuck in the '90s* since I was a kid. I didn't want it to end. None of us did. What would've happened to this show without me?"

They would've found someone else, I thought. Or they would've made Kristen or Amber the lead until they could come up with an alternate storyline they liked better. Maybe they would've followed my parents after I left, or done a spin-off with one of the half dozen popular kids at Swickley

High. Matt Hsu seemed particularly primed for comedy. He'd been in Senior Follies last fall and had people spitting their popcorn.

In Swickley, everyone was replaceable.

Mims kept rambling, and at some point she took on a strange, Oscar-acceptance-speech tone, with her saying how much it all meant to her, and how she would never forget her fans. "I know this isn't what you wanted," she said, moving closer to the camera. "There will be a vote. I promise you. I'm not leaving until there's an official vote because you are the ones who should decide."

I thought maybe that was it, that she'd just turn and go, but instead she scanned the room. She grabbed my old Jansport backpack from the floor and emptied a pile of books onto the bed, their paper-bag covers splayed open. Then she started grabbing things. When she put the Discman and a CD binder in I didn't care, but after that she took a picture frame off the dresser—a ceramic one Sara had gotten me—and shoved that in the bag too.

"What are you doing? Those aren't yours." But she kept going, picking a wizard troll doll off my bookshelf, along with a Delia's dress I'd ordered last year using money I'd made that summer at the YMCA. She started moving faster, sweeping a whole stack of T-shirts into the bag. When she went for the Lucite ring and hoop earrings on my nightstand I stood, not sure what to do. It's not like I was going to fight her.

Was I going to fight her?

Mims looked at me, then at the ring, trying to figure out

if it was worth it. The answer must've been no because she stepped toward the camera, framing herself in the center of the shot, as if she'd practiced it a hundred times before.

"There will be a vote. I promise."

Then she threw up her hand in a peace sign, making a pouty face that she must've thought was cute but was actually kind of strange. She held it there, frozen for a few seconds, maybe for a promotional still, or to give viewers one last shot to remember her by. Then she turned and left, the backpack swinging on her shoulder.

The front door opened and closed. Outside, a Swickley Alarms car pulled up at the edge of the driveway, right on cue. Mims tossed the Jansport in the back seat and slid in behind it, like she'd just hailed a taxi. The car stopped at the stop sign on the corner. Then it turned left and disappeared from view.

15

The next morning, the house was quiet. There was no bacon smell wafting up the stairs, enticing me to wake up. I kept waiting for my dad to knock. He was usually the one to tell me I should hurry and get ready for school, that I was going to be late, and why did I have to change my outfit so many times anyway? But the alarm clock ticked from six thirty to seven to seven fifteen. Nothing.

At seven thirty, I finally let Fuller out to do his business in the backyard and noticed my parents' door was still closed. My mom's purse was exactly where it had been the night before, open on the kitchen counter. I dumped kibble in Fuller's bowl. I brushed my teeth, using one of the brand-new toothbrushes we kept under the sink, because I was too afraid Mims had drooled all over my blue one. I checked the iPhone in the bathroom but there were no new messages, nothing. I put on my favorite flared jeans and J.Crew sweater and sat on the couch, not sure what, exactly, I was supposed to do.

Then I heard the horn outside.

I'd thought I'd made it clear to Amber that we weren't friends, that we weren't anything anymore, and I wasn't going to pretend otherwise. But there she and Kristen were, sitting in my driveway in Kristen's pee-yellow Volvo, which we'd affectionately named Millie. Kristen kept on with her peppy, staccato beeps, as if it were any other Monday morning. Then she spotted me in the window.

"Jess, you loser!! We know you're in there!"

I let the curtain fall shut, just as a balled-up McDonald's wrapper hit the glass.

"Are they freaking serious?" I asked Fuller.

He tilted his head to the side, his brown eyes barely visible under his shaggy bangs.

"Jessica Flynn!!" Kristen was yelling even louder now. "J-E-S-S-I-C-A!"

She leaned on the horn, letting out one long beep. That was it. I threw the door open and started down the front porch, watching Kristen's expression change as I approached her. She went from laughing to confused to nervous in only a few seconds.

"What are you doing here?" I asked.

"We're your ride to school." Amber leaned over, trying to get a better view of me. She raised her eyebrows, as if to say, *play along.*

"There's nothing you want to say to me?" I asked.

Kristen banged her palms against the wheel. "Oh god, here we go."

"We're sorry, Jess, okay?" Amber pointed to the back

seat. "Just get in."

So this was how it was going to be. A quick apology. Get over it, get on with it, then back to normal. They still expected me to hang out on Kristen's trampoline after school, and hold Amber's books in the gym bathroom, when she was fixing her lip gloss. We were still supposed to decorate each other's lockers and sign each other's yearbooks and go shopping for prom dresses together. The prop department had probably already found some vintage 1997 stretch limo that would look great on camera.

"I told you." Kristen turned to Amber. "More drama than the Real Housewives. This is going to be a shit show."

She rambled on, but I was already halfway down the driveway, grateful I'd at least worn my Doc Martens for the thirty-minute walk to Swickley High. If I was supposed to go to school, I'd go to school. The extras my age that were inside the set got credit for every class they took, accumulating them just like they would if Swickley High were real. And now that I knew that Mrs. Saetang, my AP bio teacher, had founded a rehabilitation center for sloths, and my history teacher Mr. Finegood hosted the *World 101* web series, it was all a lot more appealing than getting my GED through online courses. The virtual instructors were interchangeable, their movements clunky. The AI wasn't quite sophisticated enough to make it feel real.

As I turned up the street the Volvo reversed out of the driveway, about to follow me, but stopped at the sound of a screeching horn. A forest-green Land Rover raced down the block. Kipps was in the front seat, and he looked more like himself than Patrick Kramer, even though he was wearing the padded North Face fleece. He smiled this deranged smile and I wasn't sure if he was going to smash into the Volvo's rear fender until he swerved, pulling the car to a stop so it was angled across the street. He leaned over and popped open the door.

"Your chariot . . . awaits."

I couldn't get in fast enough. I crawled over the passenger seat, trying to get as close to him as possible, and before I could think about the cameras or the audience we were kissing, his mouth hot against mine. He shifted into park and his hands came up to my face. When I finally pulled back I realized his eyes were watery.

"I can't believe you came back," he said.

"Of course I did." I whispered it, hoping only he could hear me.

"This is all my fault. I'm so sorry, Jess, I never should've left the house that—"

"Stop," I said. "You didn't do anything wrong."

"But I didn't want this to happen."

"Neither did I, but it's okay. I'm here."

And it'll all be worth it, I wanted to say. If I could help Beyond1998, if I could get the footage they needed to go after LLP, then it would all make sense.

I leaned in, our foreheads touching. Kristen blared her horn.

"We get it! You're in love!" she yelled. "Now move your freaking car!"

Apparently we'd blocked her in. The back of the Land

Rover stuck out into the driveway. Kipps started laughing, and everything about his face was different, so much different than it had been in that clip of *'90s Mixtape* I'd seen. He wasn't the same person as he was in his kitchen with his parents, or when we were stuck in Charli's house, spending all those months in hiding.

It took a second for me to realize what it was.

He was happy.

16

You know in teen movies when a couple walks through the school, and all the other students fall back against their lockers, parting like the Red Sea? They're so googly-eyed for each other that they hardly notice that everyone's staring, wishing they were them? The scene goes all slow motion, and maybe that Sixpence None the Richer song plays, or maybe it's K-Ci and JoJo, and their fingers thread together and the light hits their faces in just the right way so they look angelic when they lean in for a kiss.

That's what it felt like when Kipps and I walked through the double doors and into Swickley High for the first time together. Ben Taylor and Alex Gonzalez stopped their make-out session to gawk at us. The kickline girls outside the auditorium giggled, and Mr. Lyle, my study hall teacher, seemed so charmed by us I almost forgot he'd been arrested this summer on a drug possession charge. It didn't matter if the scene had been rehearsed three times before we pulled up, or if they'd been given specific instructions to act like this was all normal, Kipps and me returning to set after a harrowing escape. It didn't matter if the freckly freshman who'd opened the doors for us was really Pia Jeong, a YouTube star known for her epic mukbangs.

This was our moment. This was us announcing that we were together.

"It's a bit over-the-top." Kipps's words were soft in my ear. "And a little weird?"

"But the good kind of weird."

He kissed me right then, in front of everyone. Heat spread through my chest, and I pulled him closer, threading my arm through his. My head on his shoulder. His arm around my waist. I wanted to slow time, to just walk down this one long hallway forever.

"You sure this is it?" he asked, as we hovered outside the last classroom. I rifled through my bag, past a Trapper Keeper and textbooks, looking for my schedule. When we'd pulled into the senior parking lot Chrysalis's assistant had been waiting there in a beat-up 1992 Ford Explorer. He'd had on a backwards Mets hat and JNCOs that three kids could've fit inside of. If it wasn't for the baby-blue, patent leather flight bag he'd handed me, I might've mistaken him for any other Swickley High student.

"Calc with Miss Baxter," I said to Kipps. That's what the schedule says."

I peered inside. A brunette with massive shoulder pads stood at the chalkboard.

"When do I get to see you next?" Kipps took the schedule

and read through it, then said, "Not until sixth period."

"That's too long."

I leaned against the lockers and he kissed me, his hand brushing my cheek. What was wrong with me, that I didn't care that there were millions of people watching? Why couldn't I stop? When he finally pulled away he turned down the hall, rushing to class out of habit, or maybe because even Kipps was a decent actor, pretending he needed to beat the bell.

There was only one desk open in the entire classroom, and it was right next to Kristen. Kristen, my supposed best friend, who'd been stuck behind Kipps's Land Rover the entire mile and a half on Old Country Road but had somehow beaten me to first period. I imagined her and Amber ditching the Volvo behind a dumpster and sprinting through some underground tunnel just so she could make it here in time.

"Don't ignore me. Please, Jess," Kristen whined, before I could even take my seat.

"Please what? Can we not do this?"

"Do what?"

"This fake, bullshit friend thing. Everyone knows it's an act." I gestured around the room, accidentally pointing to a scrawny boy with buck teeth, who looked terrified to be singled out. "Spare me the charade."

"And what did I do that was so horrible? Make money? Have a job?"

Kristen chewed on the end of her pencil. She'd "moved" to Swickley when she was ten, in the middle of fifth grade. I remembered the day she walked into our class, a head taller than everyone else, in her purple Umbro shorts and Sambas. It was Valentine's Day, and she looked like she belonged on a soccer field, not cutting out doily hearts with the rest of us. There'd only been one desk open, right next to me, and when Kristen had—

"This is a setup," I said, pointing at our desks. "Everything in here is set up. I wish you'd just admit it instead of making me feel like I'm going crazy."

Kristen leaned back in her chair. "You're not going crazy."

"I know I'm not."

I must've said it a little too loudly because Phil Ciani and his boyfriend turned around, along with three seniors I knew from band. I hadn't seen any of them since March and I had the sudden, weird impulse to ask Kima Johnson what happened with Jake Lefkowitz, the junior she'd taken to the Winter Formal.

"I thought your job was your podcast network," I said, unable to stop myself.

"You know about Fathom Media?"

"And '90s 4EVA. I listened to it once."

"What'd you think?" She gnawed on the pencil some more.

"Your rant on the Spice Girls was pretty funny."

"I think so too, but I'm biased," she said, seeming pleased with herself.

The bell rang. Miss Baxter introduced herself to me and started in on derivatives, which I'd technically learned through the virtual GED program, even if I hadn't retained much. As she drew a graph on the board, I could feel Kristen watching me. She'd glance over every so often, her gaze boring through the side of my head. At one point a paper football note landed next to my Doc Martens, but I just kicked it to the other side of the room. I was worried that if I read it, I might give in to the part of me that wanted everything to go back to normal, as messed up as normal was.

No one could make me laugh the way Kristen did—until I was gasping for air, my eyes wet. No one was as blunt as her, how she'd just say the thing you were thinking out loud, when most people stuffed it down, trying to be polite. She'd once told Mr. Mortimer, our health teacher, that he needed a new deodorant—but not in a mean way. Just like: *You kind of smell, dude. Get it together.* When I listened to her podcast, I'd felt this weird sense of pride. Because it was Kristen at her funniest, even if it wasn't the exact same Kristen I knew.

Our teacher had just started explaining the sum rule when the intercom crackled.

"Miss Baxter? Miss Baxter?" Mrs. Jergens, Principal Green's secretary, said it in a singsongy voice. "Will you send Jessica Flynn to the main office?"

"Right, of course." She wiped the chalk from her hands, leaving ghostly prints on the front of her pantsuit. "You heard her."

"Ooooh someone's in trouble . . ." Kristen said, and the class broke out in scattered laughs. As unreal as it all was, I still felt my stomach tense as I grabbed my bag and took the long, lonely walk to the principal's office, my steps echoing off the tile floor.

When I got there Mrs. Jergens had her feet on her desk. She was playing Angry Birds on her iPhone between bites of egg sandwich. She barely looked up as she pointed across the hall. "They're setting up in the guidance counselor's office. Something about an interview."

"I thought Principal Green wanted to see me?"

"Who?" Mrs. Jergens seemed confused, then said, "Oh, right. No."

She slingshotted the birds one after another, groaning when they missed their targets. Across the hall, the guidance offices were open, and I hadn't gotten even two feet inside when I heard Chrysalis's voice. "The light should look natural, like sun streaming in from the window. I'm playing the big sister type, the cool guidance counselor. Her friend. Her confidante." She pressed her lips together, letting a makeup artist with a blue bob dab foundation over her chin. Her assistant and Marta, the stylist, were huddled in one corner of the room.

"You're here," she said, spotting me in the doorway.

"What's this about?"

"We're going to need to close some gaps. Catch the audience up on a few things. I thought we'd create a little scene we can edit into tonight's episode so everyone isn't completely confused by your sudden romance with Patrick Kramer. Considering the last time they saw you, you were complaining about how boring he was."

"White bread. The plain yogurt kind of boring. I think that's what I said."

"Yes, that is what you said."

"You're going to be in it?"

"Thought I'd make a cameo. First time in *Stuck in the '90s* history, unless you count your eighth birthday party, when the cameras accidentally caught me crossing the street behind Regina Wallace Park."

She checked her reflection in her iPhone, then slid it back into the desk drawer. Her dark black liner was gone, and instead she was fresh-faced, with shimmery lip gloss. The brunette wig she wore had long curls like perfect coiled springs. As she stood, she gestured for me to sit on the musty tweed couch.

"Let's get this moving and get you back to school. We don't want to miss the juicy stuff," she said, then pointed around the room. "The cameras are in the psychology textbooks behind me, the desk lamp, and that light right there."

"We're not going to do this in your office?" I smoothed my hands over the couch cushions as Marta and Chrysalis's assistant slipped out, shutting the door behind them. "In the Chateau?"

"I never put it on camera," she said. "Why?"

My throat tightened. "It's just cool, that's all."

"Everyone loves Skyspace. Best six hundred thousand dollars I've ever spent."

Then she began, but she wasn't the serious, expressionless Chrysalis I'd seen on e-billboards in New York. She played the kind, understanding guidance counselor. Her hands were folded in her lap, her fuchsia manicure replaced with modest clear polish. Her words were soft and monotone, and she kept her head tilted to one side, nodding at my answers, as if she was considering everything I'd said. The first questions were basic, stuff about how it felt to be back, and if I missed the world outside the set, and if I was liking my new (old) nineties wardrobe.

"And Kipps Martin . . ."

She let the name float between us. Took a deep breath and waited.

"Yeah?"

"He's the actor who played Patrick Kramer for so long. I couldn't help but notice you two in the hall this morning. It seems like you're a couple now?"

"Yeah, I couldn't imagine my life without him."

"How did that happen?"

"I guess you go through something big together. Like, this monumental event. And I learned who the real Kipps was. Not Patrick Kramer. He's much cooler than the character he plays on the show."

"You left the set together . . . but you separated soon after?"

"We did." I slowed down, walking myself through the lies I'd already told, trying to retrace my steps. "We were helped by several people who used to work on the show. I promised I wouldn't reveal their names. And to be honest, I'm not even sure they gave me their real ones. They split us up. I was hiding out in a house in the middle of nowhere. I don't want to speak for Kipps, but those months for me were a blur. I just kept thinking that I needed to find Sara and Charli once I turned eighteen. So much of my focus was on that."

"And Kipps was focused on finding you."

"Yeah, I think so," I said. Part of me wanted to get more specific, but I didn't want to inadvertently get anyone in trouble. "We met up right after my eighteenth birthday. It was a happy reunion, that we all found each other in Maine."

"So a month ago? Isn't that a bit fast?" Chrysalis leaned forward, adjusting the hem of her corduroy skirt. When she looked up her expression had hardened, and I saw a glimpse of the Chrysalis I knew, the person who'd dragged Kipps back here against his will.

"I guess so. Yeah."

Her eyes were still fixed on me, her head tilted to one side. I couldn't tell if she knew I was lying. It felt like forever before she said, "What is the one thing you want the world to know about the real Patrick Kramer? What do you love about him?"

"He's smart, and silly and weird." I laughed. "And he's not the jock everyone thinks he is. He likes fantasy books and indie music and playing video games with his brother."

The fire rose in my cheeks. It was strange, telling everyone how much I loved Kipps, after so many months of keeping it secret. It was like a switch had flipped inside me. Now I was worried I'd never be able to stop. "He's kind of perfect."

"Sounds like he's perfect *for you*."

"Yeah."

For a moment I actually felt like she was on my side, like she was rooting for me.

"What else?" she pressed.

"He has all this random useless knowledge about animals.

Weird animals, like dugongs and tarsiers. It's actually kind of unsettling. He had three books when he was a kid and one was this animal encyclopedia, and he memorized every page."

"Dugongs?" Chrysalis smirked, as if she were genuinely charmed.

"They're the cousin of the manatee."

"Sounds like you're in love."

"With dugongs?"

"No. But nice hedge."

Chrysalis paused, waiting for me to say it.

"I do. I love him."

I'd barely finished when Chrysalis stood and pulled off her wig. She tugged her blond hair out of its bun, letting it fall around her shoulders. She tried to catch her reflection in the window but a huge circular light was just beyond the glass, shining in like an artificial sun.

"That was great. Thanks, Jess. You can head back now."

"That's it?" I asked.

"We got what we need." She combed out her hair with her fingers. "But I did want to tell you one thing. It's better if you at least try with Amber and Kristen. The audience is connected to those characters. They've been on the show for years. The fact that you have conflicted feelings about them only makes the dynamic more interesting. Besides, it doesn't play well, the girl who ditches her friends for her boyfriend."

"That's not what's going on."

"But that's what it looks like. And what it looks like is all that matters."

She threw open the door and yelled for her assistant. When I got up from the couch, my hands were sweaty. Chrysalis had barely looked at me before she'd left, and for some reason that felt like a bad sign. She'd said they just needed some clips to bridge the gaps, that was all. But I felt like I'd already said too much, that it was somehow already being used against me.

I stared at the desk drawer where Chrysalis had put her iPhone. Access to it was access to her email, her texts, her voice messages. The cameras on the bookshelf were at chest height, so I knelt down, positioning myself out of view. The drawer was empty except for the device. It was just sitting there, its face glowing with new notifications.

I was just about to grab it when I heard Chrysalis's heels clacking against the tiled floor. I pushed the drawer closed and stood as quickly as possible, turning to one of the upper bookshelves. I grabbed a copy of *Chicken Soup for the Teenage Soul* and flipped it open to a random page.

"Shouldn't you be heading to class?" Chrysalis asked as she strode into the room. She knelt and retrieved her phone from the drawer.

"This caught my eye," I said, holding *Chicken Soup* in the air.

She scrolled through her phone, checking her messages, then her eyes settled on the book. It took me a second to realize it was upside down. I fumbled to get it the right way, then slid it back onto the shelf, between *A 3rd Serving of Chicken Soup for the Soul* and *Chicken Soup for the Adopted Soul*.

"Huh," Chrysalis said, her voice flat. She glanced again

at the bookshelf, then at me, pinning me beneath her gaze. She turned and started texting as she walked out, any trace of my kind, empathetic guidance counselor gone.

17

"Who's next? You want some bean slop, or some chicken slop, or some cheesy slop?" The comedian Sandra Sanchez, also known as Lunch Lady Sandy, stood behind the counter, her hairnet halfway down her forehead. She couldn't have been more than five foot four, but she filled the whole kitchen, her high-pitched voice echoing off the walls. Charli was a huge fan. Sometimes I'd find her folded in a chair, laughing to herself as she watched one of Sandra's stand-up routines on her phone.

"I'll have . . ." I trailed off. The chicken soup looked like it had been sitting there for days, a thick gooey layer coating the top. The sloppy joe wasn't much more appetizing, though I liked the potato rolls, which were always warm and—

"Helloooooo?!" She banged a giant metal ladle against the sneeze guard in front of me. "This isn't Le Bernadin! Pick something and get on with it—there's a line, missy."

"Right." I glanced at the seven extras behind me, none of

whom I recognized. "Mac 'n' cheese. Thanks."

She heaped a ladleful onto my plate as she hummed "Stayin' Alive," shimmying her hips with the chorus. It seemed so obvious now . . . how had I never realized her schtick was too over-the-top to be anything besides a performance? How had Lunch Lady Sandy ever felt like a real person?

The cafeteria was already packed. I hadn't gotten three feet before Amber and Kristen spotted me and waved me over. Tyler was at their table, along with Leigh Weisman, a short, eternally optimistic junior who'd moved to Swickley last year and knew Amber from kickline. Nothing in me wanted to sit with them, or talk to them, but Chrysalis's voice was in my head now, and felt particularly menacing after she'd almost caught me stealing her phone.

"We saved you a seat." Amber pushed out the chair across from her with her foot.

"Since when are you three friends?" I nodded from Tyler to Amber to Kristen. I'd only caught a few episodes of *'90s Mixtape*—the ones right after I left and the ones right after Kipps returned—but the most recent ones had focused on Kipps's escape and his parents feeling betrayed.

"We're not." Tyler's lips twisted into this smug smirk. He slid his chair closer to Kristen's, then slung his arm around the back of it, playing with the ends of her long, curly hair. "We've been dating for a while now."

I watched Kristen work at the tab on her Snapple can, folding it back and forth.

"This is awkward," she finally said.

"No, it's really not." I shrugged, like no big deal, but my palms were slick against the plastic tray. Of course Tyler had started dating Kristen. He would've dated Kristen's grandmother if it meant an extra five minutes on camera. "I have to meet a friend, anyway."

"Oh yeah? What friend?" Tyler raised one eyebrow as he bit into a fry.

"Don't be a dick, Ty," Kristen muttered under her breath.

"Ignore him," Amber said.

"Already on it." I turned and cut across the cafeteria, trying my best to act like I was going somewhere. But as soon as I got into the hall I felt completely lost. It was empty except for Alex Gonzalez, the sophomore hall monitor, and two teachers I'd never seen before discussing a particularly disastrous PTA meeting.

I had no idea where Kipps was this period, and I was momentarily pissed at myself for committing to this story about meeting a friend, because no one would believe it was Alex Gonzalez. We'd only talked once, at a pep rally last year, when I'd accidentally stepped on her foot.

"Do you have a hall pass?" Alex asked.

"I'm actually uh . . ." I stared down at the mac 'n' cheese on my plate, which looked even less appealing now that it had been sitting out for five minutes. "I was going to take a break."

Alex glanced past me down the hall, as if Chrysalis might appear at any moment to officially approve it. When she didn't, Alex leaned forward, her fingers gripping the edge of the desk. "Third door on the right."

Then she went back to her marble notebook, where she was halfway through MASH. I had to give her credit—she was thorough. She had a popular bookstagram feed in real life, but here, inside the set, she was devoted to being Alex Gonzalez, the president of Girls Leaders Club and Ben Taylor's on-again, off-again girlfriend. She'd already circled Ben on her list of future husbands, but it was still TBD if they'd live in a mansion or an apartment.

I passed an art class, where a bunch of students were sketching a vase of sunflowers, then the school's darkroom. The door after that was a utility closet. Joe, our janitor, would sometimes pop in and out of it, tucking away random mops and brooms. I'd once seen him remove a freshman couple who'd been hiding in there, playing Seven Minutes in Heaven.

This was the third door on the right, but when I threw it open it looked like any other utility closet. Carnation-pink hand soap, glass cleaner, and felt erasers lined the shelves. I slid one of the bottles around, then pushed on an eraser, looking for a secret lever. It wasn't until I heard faint laughter that I went all the way to the fuse box in the back of the closet. It sounded like people were talking in the next room over. When I opened the metal box the whole wall came with it.

The corridor was only a few feet wide but Mr. Henriquez, my tech teacher, barely noticed me as I slipped past him. He was mere centimeters from Satchel Rhodes, an Instagram model they'd brought on to play the Swickley High cheerleading coach and his budding love interest.

"How have you never been to Maui?" he said, eyeing

her up and down. "We have to go. I have a beach house in Wailea."

"I'll bring my bikini." Satchel pouted flirtatiously.

The tunnel wound down to the right and opened into a break room with a long, snakelike table with chairs on either side. A glass fridge was packed with salads, sandwiches, and drinks with names like AWAKE and HYPE. Principal Green took the last bites of a salad while she scrolled on her phone. I hovered in the doorway, partially out of habit.

"You can sit down, you know," she said. "I'm not the principal of the break lounge."

"I wasn't sure . . ."

"I'm just finishing, anyway," she said, pushing back her chair. When she spotted my mac 'n' cheese she scrunched her nose. "Ohhh, ditch that. Pro tip: the Cobb salads are the best."

As I dumped the mac 'n' cheese into the trash I heard someone down the hall.

"Bro, come on . . ." A guy huffed. It seemed like it was coming from one of the dressing rooms. "Be cool. Bro. Brooooo! Brooooooo."

Principal Green checked her afro in the full-length mirror on the wall. "He's been going on for the last hour." She shrugged before ducking out. "What can I tell you? Everyone has a different creative process."

"Bro, that's my joint," the voice said. "You're being a dick. You're a dick, man. Stop being a dick."

He kept saying the same words different ways, with different inflections. I inched toward the door and pushed it open. A boy with a greasy black mushroom cut and an over-sized flannel shirt paced the edges of the dressing room. He had a hacky sack, and occasionally he'd toss it up, trying to volley it with his knees, but he kept fumbling.

"Bro, give me back my joint!" he said, pretending to grab something. As he turned he finally noticed me standing in the doorway. "Oh, it's you."

"You're . . ."

"I'm about to go on. Mr. Pataki is going to bust me for smoking a joint in the woods behind the cafeteria. It's supposed to be Kristen and Tyler who ratted, because they saw me when they were hooking up back there." Whatever response he was looking for, I didn't give it to him, because he pointed to the wall behind me. "I'm the druggie burnout."

I turned to look. The wall was plastered with headshots, so many they were even crammed together in the space above the door. The boy pointed to his, a little too proud of the black-and-white shot of him with his eyes half closed, his stringy hair parted down the center. Someone had scribbled out his name and written DRUGGIE BURNOUT in red Sharpie.

Beside that photo was a headshot of Mr. Allen, the head of the English department. He was a skinny, wannabe Kerouac type known for loaning poetry books to senior girls. CREEPY ENGLISH TEACHER was written under his photo in that same block font. That description, at least, was accurate.

"They're our roles," the kid explained. "All the extras have them. A lot of the guest stars. They're a reminder, you know. About how we fit in with the rest of the cast."

"The slut." I read the words under the headshot of Tabitha

Ford. All the senior guys had made fun of her for allegedly giving Nick Nathan a blow job in a movie theater bathroom. She couldn't go to parties without some gross dude chatting her up, thinking he was going to get laid. "That's horrible."

I instinctively looked for the red Sharpie, wanting to cross out the label. It wasn't anywhere. Right beside the photo of THE SLUT was a headshot of a girl who'd been in my gym class the year before . . . Valerie something. She always helped Miss Bianchi set up and take down the badminton net, and she ran bake sales and walk-a-thons for Habitat for Humanity and the AIDS crisis. She'd been camped out at the main entrance this morning, selling tickets to the Fall Formal at Chateau Bleu. THE GOOD GIRL, it said under her smiling photo.

"Ugh, Val Holmes." The boy noticed when I stopped to study her face.

"What about her?"

"She has such a stick up her ass. Everyone hates her."

I didn't know her well enough to know whether to laugh or to defend her. It turns out it didn't matter, because just then Val slipped into the room, decked out in a plaid skirt and crisp white shirt with a sweater vest over it. Her tortoiseshell glasses were so thick they made her look a little cross-eyed.

"Just you, Baz," she said, beelining to the clothing rack.

The boy huffed, like she was the one who'd done something wrong. He tossed the hacky sack at her, then caught it just inches from her face. "Loser."

"Takes one to know one," she hit back.

He opened his mouth to say something, then shut it again, his lips moving like a dying fish. Instead he took the fake joint from his pocket and twirled it between his fingers. He stuck it between his teeth before turning into the hall.

I could still hear him practicing his lines, his voice growing fainter as he headed toward the exit.

"Bro, come on . . . Broooo . . ."

18

Val picked over the clothing rack, her fingers skipping along the hangers as she searched for something specific. She finally found a black T-shirt with the D.A.R.E. logo, then changed into it, tucking her turtleneck into a locker. The whole time she barely acknowledged me.

"Sorry about that," I finally said. "I don't know him."

"You're lucky."

"He was just rehearsing in here when I came in."

"Ahhh," she said, raising her brows. "Like pretending to be stoned takes real effort. Baz does the same thing, anyway. Every single time." She tipped her head back, her eyes tiny slits. *"Bro. Broooo, come on. Just try it, broooo."*

"I think he offered me ecstasy at one of Jen Klein's parties?"

"Oh, he definitely did." She tucked in the T-shirt, checking her reflection in the mirror. "That was the after-school special episode in the twelfth season. You said no and walked away . . . but also didn't seem to know what it was?"

"Amber had to explain it to me after. They looked like Smarties."

"They *were* Smarties."

"Production doesn't hand out ecstasy?"

"Hard no."

She let out a small laugh, then cleaned her glasses on the edge of her T-shirt. Her eyes were much prettier than I'd thought. They were so dark they were almost black, and she had a smudge of shimmery plum shadow above each. "There were a lot of bets on that episode. Will Jessica Flynn JUST SAY NO? Will she realize they're fake? Will she tell on the burnout kid? It was like the NBA playoffs. People made brackets."

"I'm sure it was very disappointing for everyone."

"I was impressed." She shrugged, then flipped her head over, tousling her dirty-blond roots.

I turned back to the wall and studied the other headshots. Lloyd Gerber had been at Swickley High since I was a freshman. There were stories about him failing biology three different times, until Mrs. Malhotra finally passed him with a D-minus. They said the only class he ever made it through on the first try was tech. THE SUPER SENIOR, it said under his name.

The others were worse. A row of portraits that looked like runway photography were labeled THE SEXY CHEERLEADERS, with one labeled THE QUEEN BEE. A particularly skinny girl, Anna Volkov, was singled out as ANNA-REXIC. Below them was Fitz Flemming, a TikTok star who was known for lifting cars. ROID RAGE was scribbled beneath his headshot.

"Who made these? They're awful," I said.

"Chrysalis and the other producers." Val inched closer, pushing the door shut so no one would hear us.

"I get that the extras might've agreed to this . . . but it's still gross."

"I don't know, the producers seem to think it makes the show more digestible," Val said. "Good guys, bad guys. There are people you root for and against."

"The audience likes this?"

"It gets them talking. And the producers like controversy. Some people—the ones with more than two brain cells—have dissected all the different tropes. PhD candidates have written dissertations on the show. Like, what does this say about that decade that kids were afraid to come out in high school? That the president of the United States hooked up with an intern and managed to make her the villain? Does *Stuck* do a disservice to the truth, because let's be real—the nineties were racist and sexist and homophobic."

I turned back, realizing there were more. They'd labeled Claire Knox, the head of the Mathletes, THE UGLY DUCKLING, with a little aside beneath it: MAKEOVER THIS SPRING. Antoni Edwin, who played the clarinet, was THE CLOSETED GAY KID. There were freshman and junior versions of THE BULLY and THE LOSER, and I'd seen them interact dozens of times before. I'd once stepped in just before Biff Bunning flipped Mike Capezio's lunch tray.

"So they just put it up here, for everyone to see," I said. "It's so messed up."

I picked at the tape on the corners, taking them down one at a time and putting them in the trash. Val helped, but we only got halfway through them before she shook her head.

"This isn't even all of them. There's more in the other dressing rooms."

"Maybe next lunch break," I said.

Val ripped off Mr. Henriquez's headshot. THE COOL TEACHER was written underneath. ANCIENT SECRETARY was beside him, with a picture of Norma Grimm. She studied it, weighing the label before tossing it in the trash. "I guess Norma is, like, a hundred years old . . ."

It seemed especially cruel for Chrysalis to make everyone look at these labels, day after day, whenever they had to change costumes. It was like she and the other producers reveled in it, making everyone feel expendable. I could almost picture them debating who should play what role, passing around the headshots like baseball cards, trading them back and forth.

"I'm Jess, by the way." I trashed another armful of photos before extending my hand.

"Duh," she said. "And you already know I'm Val. I don't think I'm actually supposed to be talking to you? Or defacing LLP property with you?"

"They can't really stop us, though . . ." I said.

"True." Val pulled down a large Tupperware tray from an upper shelf and tucked it under her arm. "Plastic cupcakes. You've never stopped by the bake sales, so we've never needed real ones."

"I feel judged."

"You should." Val pointed a finger at me. "If I'm building a house for the homeless the least you can do is buy a freaking cookie."

"But are you really building a house for the homeless . . . ?" I tilted my head to one side, studying her. "Like where is the actual house?"

"Fair."

The door swung open, nearly knocking into me. Amber and Leigh Weisman pushed past, along with three other girls from the kickline team. Amber tried to say hi, but it seemed even phonier now that I'd seen this dressing room—and more of what the producers were doing behind the scenes.

Amber was so busy she didn't seem to notice we'd taken the headshots down. She was already pulling costumes from different shelves.

"Next scene we're in gym clothes," she said, tossing a few shorts and Swickley High T-shirts to the other girls. Soon the room was a mess of arms and legs, jeans and sweaters and skirts going everywhere, and Val and I were pressed against a wall, unsure of what to do. I knocked into one of the girls, then another, until Val pulled me back into the break room.

"It was cool meeting you. I mean, for real." Val shrugged, then opened her arms.

"We should hang out sometime," I said. "I'm in the market for new friends."

As we hugged, the Tupperware swung down by her side, the plastic cupcakes rattling.

She waved as she turned down the tunnel to leave, and I went for the Cobb salad Principal Green had raved about. It wasn't until I sat down that I felt something in my pocket.

The Tamagotchi was neon pink with tiny yellow dots on it. I glanced back, wondering if Val was still there, but Mr. Allen, aka CREEPY ENGLISH TEACHER, was coming toward me instead.

"Look who it is. Jessica Flynn." He winked, then paused in front of the fridge. "I still haven't forgotten that short story you wrote last year. You really should read some Grace Paley."

"I have read Grace Paley."

He started to say something else but I ignored him, instead staring at the Tamagotchi in my lap. A tiny digital creature was dancing on the screen. When I pressed one of the buttons it switched over to a message. IT'S SAR, it read. HIT 3RD BUTTON ASAP. I did exactly what she said, and the response was almost immediate. PERF, STAY TUNED XO.

I slipped the toy back into my pocket, keeping my hand there just to be sure I hadn't imagined it. I thought about Val's hug, how it had seemed a bit presumptuous, since we'd only just met. How it had lasted a second too long, her arm swinging down to her side, right by my hip.

This was exactly what I'd needed.

And it was Val Holmes, the good girl, who'd given it to me.

19

I couldn't remember how we'd gotten to the tree house. The minutes from the upperclassmen parking lot into Kipps's car and through my backyard were all the same, just one long obstacle course between Then and Now. Kipps fumbled with the zipper on my skirt. My mouth kept finding his. When I fell against the wall it creaked under my weight, and I pulled him down to the tree house floor.

"Shit, the mics," Kipps whispered.

We yanked off our shirts. I balled up my sweater and his button-down and threw them out the tree house window. They landed beside our backpacks, which we'd shed before climbing the wooden boards up the trunk. It was easy to get rid of the mics, but the cameras were so much trickier, hidden in the weirdest crevices and props. We ran our hands in every corner and double checked the folds of the musty blanket. Kipps even flipped through one of Sara's *YM* magazines, warped from a rainstorm, making sure there wasn't anything stuck between the pages.

"That's probably as safe as we're going to get," I said. "I checked a few days ago too."

He wore the blanket like a shawl, the ends hanging over his shoulders. He still looked impossibly cute to me, his thin, ropey torso all muscle and bone. I clasped my arms over my midsection, my bare skin prickling, overexposed in just my bra. Then he opened the blanket and brought me in.

We were kissing again. His lips worked their way down my neck. The late-afternoon sun filtered through the window, catching us under the woven fabric. When I opened my eyes it looked like we were under a disco ball, light twinkling over Kipps's nose and cheeks. He leaned against my chest.

"Ummmm . . . I still feel like someone's watching us," he whispered.

"I really hope no one's watching."

"It's kind of weird."

We tried to ignore it, using the blanket like a huge tarp, shielding us from the outside world. Kipps's hand slid down my stomach, his fingers circling my belly button, but I kept picturing clips from *The Real World* or *Road Rules*, or one of the million reality TV shows that had aired since, where the night-vision cameras caught a couple half naked, giggling and gyrating for everyone to see. There was always moaning and sloppy, slurping kisses.

"Now I'm paranoid," I said as our mouths mashed together.

We sat up, face-to-face beneath the blanket. Kipps still hadn't taken his sneakers off and his Sambas left a trail of dirt on my black tights.

"Okay, it's not kind of weird." He pressed my hands be-tween his. "It's really weird."

"I've gotten pretty good at spotting the cameras . . ."

"I'm an expert. But how can we be absolutely sure?"

"We can't. Which is creeping me out." I let out a long, staggering breath. "I feel like we're never going to have sex again. This is painful."

"Medieval rack level pain."

I leaned forward and rested my forehead against his. His shampoo was different now that he was inside the set, and his hair was always thick with product. He was starting to smell like a stranger.

My hand dug into my pocket, feeling for the plastic Tamagotchi.

"I have to tell you something . . ."

"That sounds serious."

"It is."

"You're scaring me."

Kipps barely blinked, he was watching me so intensely.

"I didn't just come back here for you." I said it as a whis-per, my lips against his ear. "There's this whole network of people who are against LLP. They call themselves Be-yond1998. Sara's been talking to them online for months."

"Beyond1998?"

"They're trying to expose Chrysalis and the other pro-ducers for everything that happened with Arthur. They went after him—drained his bank accounts, ruined any chances he had of getting another job. Basically forced him into hiding."

"He's alive?"

"Apparently. But there's another extra who disappeared. It's bad, Kipps."

"How bad?"

Our faces were just inches apart as I told him about Rae and the strike, and how she'd gone missing after an altercation with the LLP security team. I told him about the throngs of protesters that had gathered on the north side of the set. I described the woman we'd met in the sprinter van, and how I needed to upload the footage in Chrysalis's editing bay, and how Val had dropped the Tamagotchi in my pocket without me realizing it.

"See?" I said, twisting the metal chain around my finger. I almost passed the plastic toy to him but I noticed the little creature on it was dancing. The letters M-E-S-S-A-G-E scrolled past, one by one.

"What's wrong?" Kipps shifted so he could see.

"It's Sara," I said. "Another message."

I hit the button and the words appeared, blinking past because the text was so long. FLL FORML @ CHATEAU. WLL SEND DROP OFF PT NGHT OF. I read through it twice before passing the Tamagotchi to Kipps.

"She wants us to do it the night of the Fall Formal. We'll already be in the building," I said. "I'll have to make sure there aren't any tracking devices on me. Then I have to go upstairs and find the editing bay. It's apparently a closed network, or something like that. The computers in here aren't connected to the internet, the web, whatever. At least, not like most people. So I have to download the footage from the LLP server and then get back to the dance before anyone notices I left."

Kipps pulled the blanket tighter around us. "This is like *Mission: Impossible*."

"Mission what?"

"The Tom Cruise movie?" I must not have given him what he wanted, because he added, "You have to let me help you. There's no margin of error."

"I know." Just the thought of it stressed me out, that someone might catch me in the editing bay or realize what Sara and I were planning. "You don't even know the half of it. It's so much worse than we even thought. Sara's connected with all these former employees, and they all have stories that make LLP sound legitimately dangerous. They go after anyone who goes against them. They ruin their lives. They still don't know what happened to Rae. When we're in here, we're on Chrysalis's terms. She could do anything to us. She would."

Kipps pushed his fingers through his hair. "We should talk to my brother."

"It's not something we can just go telling everyone."

"Reed's not everyone. He's the only reason I haven't completely lost my mind in here. He's self-taught. Like, anything we need to do, he'll figure out how to do it. He goes deep, drops down these rabbit holes for days, then comes up and is an expert in whatever he decided to be an expert in. Reed taught himself how to build an app. He does all these virtual Spanish-conversation dinners and now he's practically fluent. He mastered the ukulele in less than a week."

"I'm weirdly impressed."

"You should be. We just have to tell him what we need."

I grabbed my bag and thumbed through the Keroppi change purse, past quarters and dimes until I found the small metal chip our contact had given me. I passed it to Kipps.

"That's the chip we're supposed to put the footage on. I've never seen anything like it."

"Reed will figure it out," he said, and shoved it into the top of his tube sock.

I inched toward the window, keeping the blanket covering my chest. My sweater was splayed out on the ground. Kipps's button-down was in a pile a few feet away.

"I guess we need to get those," he said, joining me.

"*We?* I'm in my bra."

Kipps shook his head, as if it were a personal affront. "You really want the entire world to see how skinny I am?"

"Yes. It was all part of my master plan."

"You have so many plans . . ."

He pulled me back down to the tree house floor, the blanket slipping off my shoulders. We kicked it on top of us and snuck one last kiss, hoping no one could see.

20

Val stretched out on the checkered blanket, watching Reed try to get his chin-length black hair into a top knot. It didn't matter that Reed had come out sophomore year, and that he'd broke up with his first boyfriend just three months ago, and that I'd told Val those facts at least twice. She was still staring at him like he was the TCBY toppings bar.

"Best sandcastle wins," Kipps said, kneeling in front of the blanket. We hadn't planned on going to Maple Cove after school, so he was in his jeans, sand collecting in the folds of the denim.

"Best? What does that even mean, *best*?" Reed scrunched his nose at him. "That's not quantifiable."

"They're going to quantify it. With a vote." Kipps gestured at me and Val.

"She's your girlfriend." Reed stared at Kipps in disbelief. "And they've both just met me, like, an hour ago. You're stacking the deck."

"I am not." Kipps made little trowels with his hands, dragging his fingers along the sand to form a moat. Reed was still staring at him, annoyed, then seemed to realize he was wasting time. Every second he argued was a second Kipps pulled ahead.

"I can be impartial," I said as Reed begrudgingly scooped mounds of wet sand from the water line. He flashed me a smile and then rolled his eyes, as if he didn't quite believe me.

It was fun, not being the only one giving Kipps shit. Reed was nineteen but somehow seemed much older, accepting Kipps's brotherly competitiveness with a kind of good-humored resignation. The "best" sandcastle competition had followed the "tallest" sandcastle competition, which Reed had easily won. He'd won a handstand competition too, and though I'd never say it to Kipps, I got the sense Reed was good at most things he tried.

He'd applied for a prestigious virtual university based in England on a lark, after watching a ten-hour documentary on the country and falling in love with the Thames and the Premier League and fish-and-chips and deciding he had to move there one day. He got in (of course) and then started playing soccer. He was the one who loved it, practicing every night in their massive backyard, even though Kipps was the one playing a varsity striker on the show.

I wasn't sure when or how Kipps had told Reed about our plan for the night of the Fall Formal, but he had, and I'd decided it would be less obvious if he and Val went as friends. It turns out it was maybe kind of weird for a college student who'd been in a grand total of eleven episodes to show up at a high school dance unannounced.

"How am I doing?" Reed glanced up at me. He'd only managed to make a mound of dirt so far, but Kipps already had a moat and what looked like several small buildings.

"I think you might have this," I lied. "I'm rooting for you."

"Definitely," Val added. She pressed her chin into her hands, watching as Reed dug all the way down to water, using it to shape the thing. In just a few minutes his castle had transformed into a square behemoth, with little ridges along the top.

"This is getting embarrassing for you," I told Kipps, and he was visibly flushed, trying to get his castle to look like something. Instead he decided to toss a fistful of sand at Reed, which resulted in Reed trying to kick Kipps's castle over, which then launched a full-out wrestling match.

Kipps squeezed Reed's cheeks with both hands, like he was a little baby. "Stop being so good at everything, damn it!"

Kipps and Reed rolled past us, kicking up sand in their wake. Val inched away so she wouldn't get hit. It was strange, being back here with them. I noticed all these tiny details I hadn't before. Like the waves, which you could set your watch by. They came in timed sets of two, then three, then two, and they were all the exact same height, breaking in the exact same way. The air was so still we never had to worry about the blanket getting blown away by the wind. I realized now it was because of the wall, which was close enough to the beach to give it cover. In Maine it had been the exact opposite—whenever I was by the water I had to hold on to the edge of my skirt.

At some point Val had pulled a Trapper Keeper from her bag. She was scribbling down what looked like prices, copying them from a few pages back. Every so often she'd twist her hair around her finger and let out a long, harrowing sigh.

"What's wrong?" I finally asked.

"I'm just figuring out this budget," she said, lowering her voice.

Reed had given up wrestling and was now brushing the sand from under his shirt and shorts. Kipps was grumbling about how Reed beat him in everything and Reed was gracious, reminding him that he was better at *Dirt Road*, this VR game they both liked.

"For what?" I asked.

"Expenses, bills. I'm the only one in my family who works, so I've had to get comfortable handling money. My parents have been kind of checked out," she said. "It's stressful."

I tried to make eye contact with Kipps but he and Reed were debating the merits of stealing food in *Dirt Road*, which sounded a lot like *Oregon Trail* 2.0. Part of me had wanted to let Val in on our plan for the formal, especially now that she'd be with us in the limo, but Kipps claimed it was too risky. We didn't know what she knew and how deep she was in Beyond1998, just that she'd given me the Tamagotchi. It was possible she'd done it as a favor for someone. She might not have even understood why.

"Maybe they'll promote you to a guest star at some

point? Don't they make more?" I asked.

"Not unless Chrysalis takes some special interest in me, and that's not going to happen anytime soon. Even now that we're hanging out, I still barely get any screen time," she said. "I get why all those extras went on strike, I do. I would've too if my entire family didn't rely on my salary. If that makes me a scab, whatever."

Val added up a few more bills, then subtracted the total from a bigger number. She pushed her glasses up on her nose and kept working.

"Douche alert," Kipps said.

When I turned, I didn't recognize the yellow Jeep Wrangler pulling into the parking lot. It was blasting "Semi-Charmed Life" so loud the bass buzzed and rattled. It wasn't until they pulled into a spot, nearly crushing a trash can, that I saw Kristen hanging off one of the roll bars. She shimmied and waved her arm to the music. Amber and Leigh Weisman were perched in the back seat, wearing bikini tops and cutoff jean shorts.

"That's Tyler's car?" I asked, as he turned off the engine.

"He got a huge raise when they made him a guest star," Val explained. "His lawyer negotiated all these perks. New car, bonuses, one of the private dressing rooms behind Principal Green's office."

"I don't even have a private dressing room," I said.

Val's gaze lingered on them as they all jumped out of the Jeep, Kristen laughing and tossing her hair this way and that, like she was in an Herbal Essences commercial.

"Should we go?" she asked.

"Definitely."

It wasn't a coincidence that they were here. They chose a spot only yards away from us, setting down their blankets in front of the same picnic tables where Tyler and I had made out, when we were still doing that sort of thing. Back in The Before, when I was still under the delusion that I loved him.

"It's starting to feel like they're the cool kids and we're the unpopular losers," Val said. "Shouldn't it be the other way around?"

"I definitely don't need to be on screen all the time. Let them have it." I grabbed a half-empty Doritos bag and Twizzlers and Jolly Rancher wrappers. We'd raided 7-Eleven on the way over and now I had a stomachache from all the junk food. "Let's be the Chris Kirkpatrick of '90s Mixtape. Everyone's all: Justin Timberlake is soooo hot. Ohhhh, JC. Everyone loves Lance and no one is forgetting Joey Fatone because his name is Joey Fatone. People might not be obsessed with Chris, but 'N Sync isn't 'N Sync without him."

Val bit her bottom lip, looking disturbed. "But I don't want to be Chris Kirkpatrick. Nobody wants to be Chris Kirkpatrick."

"Yeah, he sucks." Even Reed seemed in a gloomy mood now.

"It was a metaphor," I tried.

"No way." Kipps was the first one to stand. "Jess and I are the leads of the show, not them. We're not Chris Patrick."

"Kirkpatrick," I corrected.

"Whatever."

I balled up the empty wrappers and turned, cutting across to the trash can at the edge of the lot. Amber must've spotted me, because I hadn't gotten even a few feet and she was already up, hurrying along the beach. I started powerwalking like one of those moms at the Swickley Mall.

Sara was the one who'd first showed me the fan theories online about the iPhone incident, how some of the audience thought Amber had done it on purpose—literally dropping a clue—because she'd felt guilty about lying to me. There were other theories about how the scene was orchestrated by Chrysalis and LLP, that they'd decided the show would be more interesting if I started to suspect what was happening. Then things had spiraled out of their control. It sometimes felt like the whole world was conspiring to make sense of it, to convince themselves that the characters they'd grown attached to weren't just . . . really bad people.

Helene and Carter. Kristen, Tyler. Even Amber.

But I knew the truth. They were just really bad people.

My mall mom powerwalk wasn't enough—Amber reached the trash can before I did.

"You should come sit with us," she said. "Who cares about Tyler? You're dating Kipps now anyway."

"No, thanks. I'm good."

I suddenly understood why everyone loved their phones so much. It was awkward, just the two of us standing there, with nothing to scroll through or check as a distraction.

"Come on, Jess. How long are you going to be mad at me?"

She swiped her braids down in front of her shoulder, fingering one of the ends. She had on the BFF necklace I'd given her in eighth grade—a broken metal heart. The 4EVA half was in my room, hanging from my desk lamp, along with a bunch of ribbons I'd won at Girls Sports Night. I knew it was a trap, a prop placed there to manipulate me, but seeing it on her neck, I couldn't help but feel a pang of sadness. How had we gotten so far away from the fifth graders who choreographed their own Bell Biv DeVoe dance? Amber used to be my everything friend—the one I'd asked for a pad when I'd gotten my period on Field Day, the one who helped me pick out the outfit I wore for eighth grade graduation. The one who kept all my secrets.

At least, I'd believed she did.

"I have to go," I said, turning back toward the car.

"Remember that time we went to Sparkle Splash, the water park?" she called after me. I didn't want to stop but I felt myself slowing, being drawn back. "And our raft got stuck under the waterfall? And we were just getting pummeled, but we couldn't actually do anything because we were laughing so hard?"

I didn't want to look at her but I did. Her eyes were tearing up, and I tried to think of it as just more nuanced acting, that it didn't actually mean anything. I'd been there when she twisted her ankle performing at the varsity football game. I knew what it looked like when she was truly in pain.

"You can't fake that," Amber said. "And I know I've screwed up, but I'm only a few years older than you. I'm trying, Jess. I'm really trying."

"I know," I said, feeling myself soften.

"I miss you." She took a deep breath, and then her fingers moved to her necklace, tugging at the broken heart. "Please, just stay. Hang out with us."

Kipps was at the other end of the parking lot, Reed riding shotgun. Val had rolled the back window down and was now giving me one of those horror-movie looks, her eyes bugging like I was about to get hacked up by an axe-wielding psycho. They were all watching, waiting.

Maybe it was the way Amber clung to the necklace. It was a bit melodramatic, like something someone might've suggested she do. I suddenly had a vision of her in Chrysalis's office, sitting on that weird mattress couch. Two soulless producers discussing how this scene should play out. It must've been the same place where they'd talked through Sara's progressing illness, or how to set it up so I'd fire Mims myself, the cameras catching everything. Even if those fandom theories were right and Amber had dropped her phone on purpose . . . that was the bare minimum she could do to help me, and the bare minimum wasn't enough. We couldn't go back to being friends because what we'd had wasn't a friendship. It was a job for her, lying to me for all those years.

"I really have to go," I said, hurling the balled-up wrappers in the trash.

When I got back to the Land Rover Val was groaning about the bus for the extras and Darren Hardwick, who was always blowing up the tiny, three-by-three bathroom in the back. I kept trying to push it out of my head, that memory from the water park. Amber and me trying to keep our bikini bottoms on as the waterfall pounded us. Her yelling for me to help, her words broken by laughter. Us slipping and falling into the raft, water sloshing against the sides as we tried to get up.

It was useless. It didn't matter how hard I tried to unthink it. It stayed with me all the way home.

21

Kipps aimed the champagne bottle at the ceiling, his thumbs pressing against the cork. He turned it to the side, as if he were wrestling it into submission.

"It's going to explode!" Val yelled from the other end of the limo. She hid behind her clipboard, shielding her face and neck.

The cork popped, whizzing across the back seats, bouncing off the divider and landing in Reed's lap. We were celebrating already, filling each of the champagne flutes with the legal, nonalcoholic champagne the producers had provided for the night. The limo turned into the Chateau's long, winding driveway, and I slid across the leather seat, my shoulder smashing into Kipps's.

"This driver is horrible," I said.

"It's on autopilot," Kipps whispered. "All the cars inside the set are now . . . since my great Land Rover escape last year. Everyone just pretends to drive them. That dude has been talking to his girlfriend for the past half hour . . . you didn't notice?"

I leaned forward, watching the guy through the tinted glass. His fingers were pressed to his ear and he kept smiling, then laughing, and I swore he mouthed *awwww baby, awwww baby*, though I couldn't be sure.

Reed raised his glass across the limo, trying to get our attention. "It's going to be an epic night," he yelled over the music. "Epic."

He and Kipps were both in tuxes, and they'd gelled back Reed's chin-length hair so it stayed tucked behind his ears. The costume department put me in a long red dress with a black slip over it. Tiny beaded flowers covered every inch of the sheer fabric. To Val's dismay, they wouldn't let her go without her glasses, but they'd styled her dirty-blond hair with a dozen butterfly clips, little wisps framing her small, heart-shaped face. Val was on the planning committee, and she'd brought along a huge jar filled with raffle tickets, which she'd strapped into a seatbelt, as if it were her date. She had two cardboard boxes of party favors—blue votives with gold moons and stars to go with the Moondance theme. Even now, she kept checking her clipboard, making sure she had all the candles and ribbons that went with them.

As we pulled up to the front entrance, Kipps and Reed helped Val load her boxes onto the curb. I hung back to check on the Tamagotchi in my purse. Sara had gotten information that the editing bay was somewhere behind Chrysalis's desk, and she'd given me a code to get into the elevator, and then the office, when no one was there.

Chrysalis, executive producer turned guidance counselor, was scheduled to make a cameo at the dance between eight and ten. We would have to get upstairs, get the information, and return in that window.

W8 4 DISTRCTION, said the newest message in the Tamagotchi. WLL B OBVIS. ULL NEED CODE 4811. The person helping with the distraction tonight had to be working with Beyond1998, though I couldn't imagine who it could be. Val didn't seem to know anything about the plan, and besides, she'd already risked so much.

"You coming?" She peered into the limo. I must've hesitated for a half second, because she nodded at the Tamagotchi before I slipped it back in my purse. "You're obsessed with that thing."

"It's just a nervous habit," I tried. "I never had one as a kid."

She hugged the jar of raffle tickets to her chest as I slipped past her. I could barely see Kipps and Reed behind their boxes. They moved in a coordinated dance, circling each other as they pushed through the double doors, keeping their stacks perfectly balanced. Another stretch limo pulled up behind us and a bunch of junior girls in poufy dresses spilled out. I spotted Lindsay DiNardo smoking a cigarette behind a bush, emerging every so often to make sure none of the chaperones had come outside.

"This is why I wanted to get here early," Val said, hustling into the foyer. "I have to set up three hundred votives in ten minutes."

"We'll help you." I followed her to the entrance table

where Cindy Kim was checking everyone in. Kipps and Reed put the boxes down beside it.

"Cindy!" Val clasped her hands together. "So sorry I'm late. What can I do?"

Val didn't say it was my fault, but she didn't have to. My parents had made us take a dozen photos in front of our house, and then a dozen more in front of the limo, and then my mom had touched up my lipstick and hair and mascara before finally letting us go. I bent down and started unpacking the party favors with Kipps and Reed, but Val waved us off.

"It's fine, it's fine," she said. "I'll do it. I'll meet you inside after we check everyone in."

"A bunch of freshmen showed up," Cindy said, glancing at a particularly sad group of boys by the bathroom. One of them had on a suit that was two sizes too big. "I keep trying to tell them it's the *upperclassmen* Fall Formal, but they won't listen."

"You can't be here!" Val said it two octaves too high, clapping and smiling like a cheerleader. "Seriously, you have to go."

We moved past her into the empty ballroom, where the DJ was already blasting "Gettin' Jiggy wit It," which Sara had joked was the most grating part of living in 1998. Navy and gold balloons rose from the center of every table, confetti clinging to their insides. The chaperones lingered at the edges of the room. Mr. Henriquez was in black suspenders and a purple striped tie. He kept spinning and reaching out his hand, urging Satchel Rhodes to join him in this shimmying side step, and I wasn't sure what was real and what wasn't—he seemed that desperate to get her on the dance floor.

"I haven't been to a formal . . . ever." Reed hadn't even made it ten steps before stopping, his arms folded tight against his chest. "Are they usually this weird?"

Maybe it was the strobe lights, the electric blue and white beams that traced the floor and ceiling in menacing arcs, as if they might cut us in half, lightsaber style. Or maybe it was that with only a handful of kids, the ballroom felt cavernous and cold. Normally I would've complained or made a joke about it, but I felt for my necklace, remembering the mic there. We had to at least pretend to have fun for the next hour.

"It'll fill up soon," I tried. "Let's stake out a table."

Within ten minutes Kipps and Reed were tossing popcorn into the air, seeing how high they could throw it and still catch it in their mouths. It wasn't the super romantic Fall Formal I'd imagined, when I'd started imagining things like that, but somehow it fit. Kipps lowered his head to get one but I intercepted it, eating it myself.

"Awww, sneak attack!" Kipps grabbed a handful from the bowl.

"Aren't those your friends?" Reed nodded to the back of the room.

The varsity soccer team had arrived in one big swell. Dozens of seniors assembled like birds, perching on the antique furniture. Ben Taylor sat on the back of a chair, his heels planted on the seat. A few girls huddled over the couch, oohing and ahhhing at Lynn Ford's corsage. Together, they looked like they were posing for an oil painting, lit by the chandelier overhead. Looking back, they'd probably always been posing, but it was hard to imagine Kipps ever being one of them.

"I guess?" Kipps said.

They must've felt us staring, because Ben Taylor turned around midsentence. He paused as if he were weighing whether to come over.

"Let's dance?" I said, standing.

"I hate dancing." Reed stiffened at the word. "I feel like everyone's watching me."

"Well, everyone kind of is." Kipps shrugged.

But Reed followed us onto the floor anyway, and as soon as we made it into the center of the crowd we were invisible, and the music was too loud for anyone to hear what we were saying. Reed didn't dance as much as step to the right and the left, on repeat, and I didn't realize someone could simultaneously be so cute and so awkward. Kipps seemed to revel in it, how at ease he was in comparison, spinning beside us and then doing this snake motion with his arms.

Kipps and I made a Reed sandwich, shielding him on both sides, and at one point we were jumping up and down, our hands in the air, and it felt ordinary enough that I nearly forgot why we were there. I kept catching glimpses of Kristen, Tyler, and Amber. They'd formed a circle in front of the DJ, and they exploded in cheers when he played "Groove Is in the Heart." Leigh Weisman and Amber did part of a kickline routine, and even with Mims gone, I couldn't shake the feeling that I'd been replaced.

"She's here . . ." Kipps's lips were right next to my ear. At first I didn't know what he meant, but then I saw Chrysalis's huge, curly wig across the room. She stood beside the back doors, wearing a black evening gown with glittering rhinestones around the collar. Even I didn't immediately recognize her, that's how well she blended in, her mocha lipstick so perfectly nineties.

I tugged on my necklace, breaking the clasp and letting it drop to the floor. It disappeared under a crush of feet. Reed and Kipps had mics on their tux jackets, but those would be easy enough to shed at some point. As we danced Kipps would occasionally glance over at Chrysalis, waiting for whatever distraction Beyond1998 had planned. Ali Marks and Ally Horowitz had commandeered the photo booth. Baz and a few of the other extras who played his fellow druggie burnouts lingered at the refreshments table. One was compulsively eating cheeseballs and the other had a Fruit by the Foot hanging out of his mouth. It looked like a yellow and red lizard tongue.

We were still dancing when we heard the first scream. I turned, and half of the students had receded from the ballroom floor, staring at a body on the ground. At first I just saw a set of legs beyond the crowd. When I took a few steps I noticed the suspenders and striped purple tie. Mr. Henriquez was splayed out on his back. A few members of the varsity football team had caught him under his arms and were easing his head to the ground.

Satchel Rhodes knelt down and pressed her palm to his cheek. "He just fainted," she said. "He was just talking to me and he fell back."

Chrysalis cut through the dance floor. "Is he breathing?"

He blinked, then his head rolled to one side. He seemed genuinely shocked to see everyone staring down at him. "I don't know what happened."

"You said you were feeling dizzy." Satchel worked at the end of her long mermaid braid, tugging it nervously.

"Is this real?" Kima Johnson said to no one in particular.

"Yes, it's real." Chrysalis moved in. "Shut off the cameras. Let's get him out of here and then we'll run it all again. This is a mess."

Mr. Henriquez tried to prop himself up on his elbows. "I feel fine, Chrysalis," he said. "I must've just fainted. I didn't eat a lot today but I'm okay."

"Tony, you know the rules. We need to bring a doctor in for liability reasons. You're going to need a full workup." Chrysalis checked her watch, then scanned the back of the ballroom. She pulled out her phone and started texting furiously. "Amber will call the ambulance."

Reed peeled off his tux jacket and put it on a nearby chair, waiting for Kipps to follow. Sara had said in her message that the distraction would be obvious, and this felt like it couldn't be anything other than that. I just didn't expect Mr. Henriquez, tech teacher and international action star, to be the one responsible.

I moved behind a large pack of juniors so no one would notice when we peeled off from the group. Kipps, Reed, and I made our way toward the double doors closest to the elevators. Kipps tossed his tux jacket over a couch, then pulled off his cuff links, which were also mic'd. He tucked them into his tux pocket and we were almost there, right at the doors, when Val approached, hugging her raffle ticket jar.

"I was looking for you," she said. "What happened? Who is that?"

Kipps and Reed kept walking, barely acknowledging her as they slipped into the hallway. I couldn't not stop, though. I couldn't not respond.

"It's Mr. Henriquez . . ." I said, glancing back to the dance floor.

"You're leaving?" Val craned her neck, trying to catch a glimpse of Reed or Kipps as the doors swung closed. "We're going to draw the raffle soon. Don't tell anyone I told you, but you're going to win a dinner for two at Tavern on the Green in New York City. It's supposed to be an upcoming storyline, this whole romantic night with you and Kipps, being back in the city after your dramatic escape. It was—"

"Don't worry, I'll make sure we're back in time," I said.

"You definitely have to be." She pushed her glasses up on her nose, her eyes wide.

"I know." I scanned Val's face. I wasn't sure how much she knew about what was actually happening, and it was frustrating not being able to just tell her. "I want to get some air. Kipps and I . . . we have to do *a thing*."

"*A thing*?" Val gave me this sly, half smile, like I'd said something scandalous. "Right."

"Just cover for us? We'll be back in a bit."

Val nodded, but as we left she looked a little lost, standing alone in the center of the ballroom. If it wasn't for Kipps's paranoia, I might've told her to just ditch her mic and come.

When I got to the lobby I heard the ambulance's wail getting louder as it sped up the driveway to Chateau Bleu. Its lights flashed, red and white reflections dancing across the front windows. Kipps and Reed were already halfway down the hall. I followed, ignoring the paramedics as they stepped out onto the curb and unloaded the stretcher.

Now that they were here, the clock was ticking.

22

It felt endless, the numbers lighting up one by one, as the elevator climbed to the Chateau's top floor. When the doors slid open the waiting room was so dark I couldn't see more than a few feet ahead of us. I moved to the office's entrance, entering the code Sara had given me to bypass the scanner so I didn't have to press my thumbprint against the glass. Two beeps, and then we heard the deadbolt turn.

The office felt different without Chrysalis there. Quiet. Calm. The town spread out beyond the glass, treetops and roofs and stray headlights cutting through the night. We split up, circling the suite, and Kipps and I went to the far wall behind her desk. Kipps pressed his palms against it to see if it would give way. Reed had brought a fob he'd ordered online. He'd watched dozens of videos and somehow learned how to convert it into a universal key, which he'd hoped we could use to find the secret door. He moved the gray plastic button along the baseboards and over the oil painting, waiting to hear another beep.

"Our Beyond1998 contact didn't know where the editing bay is," I said, going to Chrysalis's desk. "But it's supposed to be here somewhere."

Two of her four screens were on, but they were just glittering gray squares with FILMING PAUSED written across each. Kipps checked the far wall beside the entrance, then under the couch, running his hand along the floor to see if there might be a secret lever or release button like some of the set's houses had.

"Don't touch the keyboard," Reed said, his voice louder than it should've been. "A lot of the high-end ones can read your fingerprints. It'll know immediately you're not Chrysalis."

"I wasn't going to," I said, which was a lie, but I felt stupid for not registering there were probably a dozen invisible safeguards in place so no one other than Chrysalis could get onto her computer. Reed was still checking the walls with the fob when Kipps came up beside me.

"Isn't this from *Clueless*?" he said, and before I could stop him, he reached for the fuzzy pink pen in the glass holder, squeezing the top of it. I stiffened, waiting for an alarm to sound, but instead the wall behind us slid back, revealing another office. "Oh, shit."

Reed turned, looking from Kipps to the open door. "You did that?"

"Sorry, dude."

"Don't be. This is where the real fun begins." Reed grabbed a pair of thin black gloves from his pants pocket and pulled them on, adjusting the band around his wrists.

"Not too much fun. We should be back downstairs in ten minutes," I said.

"Genius can't be rushed." Reed settled into one of the sleek leather chairs behind the desk, his gloved hands resting on the keyboard.

"But maybe genius can be encouraged . . ." I said. ". . . to work very quickly?"

One whole wall was covered with screens, dozens projected like a glittering veil. The four labeled CHATEAU BLEU were dark, with FILMING PAUSED scrolling across. My mom and dad were on another, in real time, having an argument. My mom was yelling but I couldn't hear what. The cameras outside Swickley High were recording, too. A swarm of underclassmen darted forward, launching rolls of toilet paper into the air. They twisted and rippled through the tree branches like birthday streamers. A freshman I recognized from my study hall had a bottle of shaving cream. He scrawled CLASS OF 2002 across the front entrance.

"They have a camera on our parents," Kipps said, pointing to another screen, where a couple was watching television. The way they were framed it was like the camera was inside the set, the light flickering over their blank faces. They both looked so innocuous in their pajamas, it was hard to connect them with the people I'd seen Kipps fighting with on the show, the ones who'd forced him to have lunches with Chrysalis to discuss how to be a more appealing heartthrob. Last year they'd insisted he wear that stupid padded North Face fleece, after the protein diet and weight-lifting plan they'd put him on had failed miserably.

"They're banking footage all day long, every day," Reed said, and he'd already somehow gotten into a list of files on another screen, swiping at the air with his index finger. He had the tiny silver chip Skeletor had given me, and he pressed it into a circular groove in the keyboard. In an instant two images of Rae were on one of the screens, a profile and another of her smiling straight ahead. Reed typed something into the keyboard and then a progress bar appeared, slowly loading 1 percent, then 3 percent.

"No, no, no . . ." I said, looking at the numbers underneath the bar. "We don't have two hours and eleven minutes."

"It always says that." Reed pulled up another window. His fingers moved over the keyboard, typing a set of indecipherable prompts. "I've set it up to scan Rae's face, and match it to any footage found on that day—February twenty-third—after three p.m. That should cut down on the files we have to pull."

A computerized grid climbed over Rae's features. Within seconds, two different clips popped up on the screen in front of him. One was a video of Rae walking down a hallway in Chateau Bleu. The carpeting had this trippy geometric pattern that was unmistakable. It was only a few seconds long and her steps were steady and sure. Nothing about it seemed odd.

"There's this," Reed said, pointing to it, "at three eighteen. But then the cameras must've been turned off. They have them everywhere in here. But nothing else was recorded until almost five o'clock."

He clicked into the other video. It was twelve seconds. The camera was perched above the scene, looking down on a mostly empty parking lot. Rae was in the same outfit she'd had on at Chateau Bleu as she crossed to one of the bus stops the extras used.

"It's the lot behind the Tower Records." I recognized the garage entrance where the producers parked. "She must've left from this exit. It looks like she's trying to get a shuttle out."

Rae was facing the camera and she looked annoyed. She was practically running, holding her purse strap with two hands. She'd almost reached the bus stop when a car appeared at the edge of the frame. Two men got out, blocking her path. She tried to sidestep one and he caught her at the waist.

"LLP security," I said, pointing to the black polo, which was more obvious as the man turned. Rae ducked under his arm. The other one rushed at her and then Rae was on the ground, kicking at them and trying to wriggle free. Her mouth was moving but we couldn't hear what she was saying.

"There's no audio?" I asked.

"No, but I might be able to use the lip reading function." He hit a few buttons, but only three words popped up.

HELP, SOMEONE! THEY'RE—

One of the security guards pressed the Taser to her leg and she fell over, writhing with pain. Then they pulled her out of the frame. I kept waiting for something else to happen, but that was it. The clip ended.

"That's the last footage of her inside the set," Reed said,

checking through the video files to make sure he'd gotten the dates right. "That's it."

"This is really, really bad." As soon as I said it, the editing bay felt smaller, claustrophobic, the walls closing in on us. There was no way to argue with those last seconds of video.

I turned back, staring into the dim office, worried Chrysalis might somehow know we were here. The moonlight filtered in through the floor-to-ceiling windows. From where we were standing I could see a narrow stretch of the perimeter wall surrounding the set, just beyond the Anderson baseball fields.

Reed started closing out of different screens, getting us back to the scenes playing out across the rest of Swickley. "I just have to put this all on the chip . . ." he said.

"We have to leave tonight," I said, trying to keep my voice even. "As soon as humanly possible."

"What about our parents?" Kipps asked.

"When this story breaks, it's all over. We just have to get the file to Beyond1998," I said.

"Mom and Dad aren't the ones who broke into Chrysalis's office," Reed said. "Jess is right. This is way worse than I thought. We can't stay. If Beyond1998 can get us out, we have to go."

Kipps bit the side of his lip nervously, his foot tapping out the seconds. He still wanted to please them, even if it meant putting himself in danger.

The silver chip was nestled into a groove in the keyboard. On-screen, the progress bar reached 87 percent. I kept wondering how long it would take for Mr. Henriquez to be put into the ambulance. The dance would soon return to normal, and Val would soon step onstage and call out my name. The cameras were still off, but that didn't mean people hadn't registered that we'd snuck away, that we were missing.

It already felt like we were out of time.

23

The upload or download or whatever Reed was doing was taking forever. I checked the Tamagotchi out of habit, and because I needed something to do with my hands that didn't involve shredding my cuticles. The MESSAGE alert was scrolling past. It was an immediate relief, knowing Sara was out there, writing to me. That we were still connected.

"We have the drop-off point," I said, reading the text. "She wants us to go to the last booth in the diner. There's someone there who will get it to her."

"The *diner*?" Kipps said. "So we're supposed to sit around, munching mozzarella sticks and hoping Chrysalis and her goon squad don't come kill us?"

"I usually went to the diner after school stuff with Amber or Tyler. Dances. Football games. That's probably why she chose it—it won't be weird," I said, but I could already feel the panic setting in. I hadn't wanted to say it, but now Kipps had, and we couldn't go back. *Come kill us.* It was starting to feel like a real possibility, that LLP could do whatever they wanted without any consequences.

There were a grand total of two buttons on the Tamagotchi. One cleared the existing messages, and the other was an improvised keyboard. It was painful how long it took to type every word when you had to scroll through the entire alphabet for just one letter. I immediately regretted leaving my iPhone in the bottom of the Caboodle, but Reed said everything had a GPS tracker on it, and they were probably using it to follow my every move. I'd only managed a K and a NEED HLP SOS, CANT STAY before Reed wheeled back in his chair.

"This doesn't seem good . . . there's something here about a game," he said, pointing to a 3D rendering of my bedroom, and another that looked like the Swickley High cafeteria. "An immersive VR experience. Some kind of on-line marketplace?"

He turned to Kipps and me, but neither of us had any idea what he was talking about. I'd heard of a *Stuck in the '90s* board game. But the only immersive VR experiences I'd played were like the World in a Box.

"I don't know what that is . . ." I said.

Reed clicked into another file, and there were more images. They had a 3D rendering of the 7-Eleven we went to after school. When he hovered the mouse over the bags of Doritos or Baked Lays there were different amounts, but the currency was all in pogs. Most of the bags of chips cost only two pogs, but Cool Ranch Doritos were three.

"Why would they make you pay in pogs?" Kipps asked.

"That's bizarre."

"It's easier to spend money that way," Reed said. "If they told you what you were actually paying . . ." He went into another sheet where there were lists of different items and how much the user would be charged for it. "Ninety-nine cents for a bag of virtual chips that you can't even eat . . . who would do that?"

I leaned over, looking at the prices. While you were inside the experience, nearly everything cost money. Admission to Adventureland was fifty pogs, which was twenty-five dollars. They charged you ten pogs to get into Maple Cove. Everything on the menu at the diner had a price. You couldn't even use the school vending machines without being charged. "You're spending money every second you're inside the game."

"It doesn't look like you have to pay it," Kipps said, studying another document. "You can open a *Stuck in the '90s* credit card."

"There's all this crap in the user agreements. You could spend your whole life paying off debt you've accumulated inside," Reed said. "They're trying to pull in loyal fans of the show. They send you the game and prop kit, which are both free, but as soon as you're in the world you could spend hundreds of dollars in just a few hours. Every time you play you're just going deeper into debt."

"This is evil," I said.

"Save those files," Kipps said. "We should share those with Beyond1998 too."

"On it."

Another bar came up on the screen and it felt endless, watching and waiting as everything loaded. When it finally finished, Reed twisted the silver chip out of the keyboard, handing it to me. I tucked it into my bra as we went back out into the office, trying to recreate the scene exactly as it was when we'd walked in. I slid the pink pen back half an inch, watching the editing bay seal off from the rest of the room.

"Sixteen minutes," Kipps said, checking his watch. "Bet they barely missed us."

"Let's hope," I said.

The dim waiting room was a relief, and as we stepped into the elevator I looked at the Tamagotchi again, wishing Sara would respond. Even if Reed could get us past the perimeter wall with his universal key, we'd need Charli or someone from Beyond1998 to retrieve us. We couldn't repeat what had happened last March, when Kipps and I had tried to leave on our own. Chrysalis and her team had had months to review the security protocols. They'd be prepared this time, and if they found us with those files . . . if they knew what we had just done . . .

We were silent, standing in the elevator like strangers, staring at the lights that counted down each floor. As soon as the doors opened I noticed the carpeting, the geometric pattern we'd seen in the footage of Rae. Kipps noticed too. He nodded to the far corner of the hallway. The camera that had captured her was there. With each step I imagined her taking the same one, not knowing what waited for her on the other side.

As we approached, the ballroom was humming with people. We reached the double doors just as paramedics were rolling Mr. Henriquez out on a stretcher. "I'm fine, really," he said. "This is ridiculous. Come on, man."

As the paramedics swung open the double doors, Mr. Henriquez turned, and for a brief moment his eyes met mine. He winked, and to anyone else it would've seemed like a subtle hello. *Jess Flynn, lead of* '90s Mixtape. *What's up?!* But it took on new meaning now, especially since he was one of the most famous guest stars. I couldn't remember the last time he even acknowledged me.

"Perfect timing," Kipps said, as we made our way into the ballroom. I could tell he was nervous, though. He pushed both hands deep into his pants pockets, gazing straight ahead. Reed retrieved his tux jacket from the chair and slung it over his shoulder. We blended in with the rest of the crowd, who'd shed various layers in the time since we'd left. Chris Arnold had taken off his jacket and shoes, and now his massive frame was stretched out across a dainty antique couch as he twisted and turned, trying to nap. A bunch of extras sat against a wall, high heels strewn about the carpet. A dozen iPhones had miraculously appeared, retrieved from secret pockets and the false bottoms of purses, and now the extras stared at them, their faces glowing with eerie blue light.

I adjusted my strapless bra, letting my thumb graze the chip just to be certain it was still in place. Everyone had split off into groups, but not the ones I would've expected. Alex Gonzalez was supposed to be dating Ben Taylor, and instead she was sitting with Jamal Harris, the drum major of the marching band, their foreheads touching. Two of the cheerleaders were hanging out with Kim Katz, who'd gotten so drunk at one of Jen Klein's parties that production had held an intervention after, and she'd spent the next three months at a rehab facility in North Carolina. Even Bill Gorski was different. Usually everyone was annoyed by him, but now he held court with half a dozen upperclassmen, who doubled over in laughter whenever he spoke.

"I don't see Chrysalis," I whispered, as we made our way to an empty table. Kristen and Amber were still there, but they were both on their phones. Amber kept ducking in and out of the ballroom. Neither of them looked at me. Were they just busy, or did they somehow already know what we'd done?

"I'm glad we took a walk." Reed buttoned his tux, reminding us his jacket was back on and his mic was recording again. "This is getting weird."

"Since when are Alex and Jamal dating?" I tried to make my voice seem light, casual.

"About a year. Jamal is Rich Harris's son, the famous singer?" Kipps was being generous, posing it as a question, even though he knew I'd missed most of the music from the past forty years.

Just then Amber hung up the phone and cut across the ballroom, clapping her hands above her head. She looked much older than everyone else, more self-assured. At a certain point she'd shed her heels and was now barefoot in shimmery nude tights.

"We're calling it for tonight." Amber turned around as

she said it, addressing the entire room. "We've lost too much time now. They're sending the buses back for you. We're scrapping the Fall Formal storyline and running a day in the life episode."

"We're still getting paid, right?" Mr. Hill, a substitute teacher, asked.

"Yes, you're still getting paid for your hours," Amber said.

A few people groaned as they collected their things. One girl said something about her dress, and it all being a waste. I kept waiting for Amber to look directly at us, but she started texting, jabbing at her screen. Kristen was still on the phone as the extras and guest stars gathered their things and filed out. I kept telling myself they were just busy, that they had to get two hundred people out of the set, but the littlest things were making me worry.

Kipps, Reed, and I slipped into the foyer. Hundreds of blue and gold votives were assembled on the table, but neither Cindy nor Val were there. They must've gotten on one of the buses already. The jar of raffle tickets was sitting on the curb next to two crushed Coke cans, the only remaining relics of the night.

24

"No word yet?" Kipps turned back, his face half in shadow.

I checked the Tamagotchi again, but nothing had changed since the last message about the drop-off point. "She's going to need time," I said. "We just go in, sit down like everything's normal, drop the chip, eat some food. Done."

"I could use some onion rings," Reed said.

He'd ripped the mic'd button off his jacket as we crossed the parking lot, passing the wood-paneled truck that belonged to Melvin, the diner's cashier. The Cresthollow Diner looked more like a giant cake than a restaurant, with red and blue neon piped around the domed roof. Most things in Swickley closed right at six, when the extras and guest stars left for the day, but the diner was one of the few places that stayed open around the clock. Craft services used it in the early mornings to provide breakfast for the crew.

The windows radiated fluorescent light. Melvin was inside, polishing the front counter.

"Melvin is our Beyond1998 contact?" One of Kipps's muscle pads had slid to his elbow, making it look like he had a strange arm growth. "He hates us."

"Or maybe it's the couple in the back," I said. Two junior girls sat in one of the booths, holding hands as they flipped through the jukebox. The producers had already moved a few extras over from the formal, mainly the musical theater crowd, who were known for spontaneously erupting into *Les Mis* songs.

"Casual. Cool," Kipps said, and I wasn't sure if he was reminding himself or us, as we bounded up the front steps. He strode in and immediately gave Melvin his hand for a high five, which was maybe the most conspicuous thing he'd ever done. "Melvin, my dude!"

Melvin threw the dishrag into a bucket of sudsy water, but didn't even crack a smile. He gave us three thick menus and gestured around the diner. "You know the drill. Wherever you'd like."

I'd always associated the diner with Kristen, since her stepmom's family had owned it for thirty years—or at least had pretended to. Sometimes Amber and I would study there while Kristen was working. She'd bring us heaping plates of fries, our textbook pages smudged with grease. It was the place to be after the Homecoming dance or the Swickley Senior Follies, the tables filled with notoriously bad tippers (Kristen had once gotten seven dimes from the boy's JV basketball team). I passed our regular booth by the window and instead went to a U-shaped one in the back. Kipps slid in beside me and held the menu so it covered his face.

"I'm starving," he said, in a voice like death.

"Me too." Reed's eyes darted to the front of the diner.

Melvin was suddenly beside the booth, rubbing his greasy forehead with his fingers. His horrible hygiene usually bothered me, but I was too distracted by my heart banging inside my ribs, my hands so shaky I had to steady them on the table.

"You know what you want?" He didn't look up from his pink notepad.

Kipps ordered onion rings and I ordered a triple-decker BLT sandwich, which was my usual, even though I wasn't hungry. Reed got a chocolate shake and Melvin scribbled it all down, then dropped the check at the edge of the table. It wasn't until he was back behind the counter, hanging the carbon copy in the kitchen window, that I noticed the last line. His handwriting looked more like an EKG than actual letters, but it was just legible enough.

ONION RINGS
BLT SANDWCH
CHOC SHAKE
LEAVE UNDER SALT

I pretended to adjust my bra and pinched the chip out, sliding it onto the table. Kipps and Reed flipped through songs, and it was calming, the *fwick fwick* of the turning metal sleeves. Reed was defending Sheryl Crow so fiercely it felt like he knew her. I pretended to play with the shakers, then covered the chip with the salt. Within minutes, Melvin came back with a tray of salts and peppers, and traded out ours, tilting them to see how much was left in each. Then he pushed through the swinging stainless-steel door behind us into the kitchen.

Grumpy, greasy Melvin. Melvin, who literally whistled while he worked, which was so annoying that Kristen had refused to be on any of the same shifts as him. It seemed so obvious now, that he'd always been against the producers, that his hatred of us was too convincing to fake.

As soon as Kipps and Reed stopped debating the merits of "Favorite Mistake," they fell silent, and I could tell the heaviness of the night had returned, that uneasy feeling that you could only forget if you were completely absorbed doing or saying something else. Melvin dropped our plates and then gave the slightest nod to the door, as if I should follow him into the back.

"I have to use the bathroom . . ." I was already up before I finished the sentence.

Melvin didn't turn around when I pushed into the hall, past the women's room and into the storage closet, which had actual supplies in it, like paper sacks of sugar and flour. It was L-shaped, cutting back and to the right, with shelving that housed all the additional napkin holders and silverware. For a second I wasn't sure where Melvin had gone, until I heard him behind me. He'd maneuvered in front of the door and was now standing there, blocking me in.

"At long last, our star has arrived . . ."

My body reacted to that voice, everything in me going cold. Chrysalis appeared at the other end of the room, sans guidance counselor getup, her eyes now lined with that familiar thick black pencil. She leaned over a stainless-steel desk, where a screen was playing the first clip of Rae entering Chateau Bleu. She shook her head, then turned it off. "You were quite the little techie tonight, Jess. I was wondering what you and your friends were doing in my office. I'm actually kind of impressed."

"I saw you get into the elevator. You lied to me." Val stood beside Chrysalis. She was still in her formal dress, but her hair had come undone, frizzy wisps falling down her neck.

"For a good reason," I said. "You don't know how bad it is, Val. Chrysalis, LLP, they—"

"She doesn't care." Chrysalis leaned on the edge of the desk, studying me. She plucked the chip from the keyboard, turning it between her fingers like a coin. Melvin must've given it to her as soon as I'd handed it off. "Val knew you were doing something you weren't supposed to, and she let me know. That's the kind of loyalty I need from my people."

"I'm not your people," I said.

"That much is clear." Then Chrysalis turned, waving Val off. "You can go now. We'll be in touch soon. Kristen will get you set up in your new role on Monday morning."

Val seemed particularly pleased with herself as she passed me, and I could only imagine what kind of recurring part they'd given her, now that she'd shown she'd do anything for the show. This whole time I'd thought I was the one putting Val at risk. I'd felt so protective, not wanting to tell her too much, or involve her in Beyond1998 any more than she already was. But she must've been playing both sides, pretending to help Beyond1998 while reporting back to LLP.

Melvin followed her out, leaving Chrysalis and me alone in the storage closet. She hadn't brought the LLP security team, and I tried to find a vague sense of comfort in that. If she wanted me dead, I would've been dead already. That, and she couldn't explain away my disappearance like she could an extra on the show. As self-involved as they were, my parents would notice if I was gone. The audience would need a compelling story. They'd want the minute-by-minute details of what had happened to me.

"I want to show you something," Chrysalis said, holding out her phone. She scrolled through a Zing feed I didn't recognize, stopping on a video with the headline BREAKING NEWS: SARA FLORES AND CHARLI DEAN QUESTIONED IN CONNECTION WITH LLP DATA BREACH. The camera was circling overhead, and then the drone dropped down and flew right past Sara and Charli, catching their faces in profile. Charli hugged Sara's shoulder as they walked into a stone building, flanked by police officers. Underneath the video were dozens of likes and comments, with one thread saying Sara and Charli were "out for revenge" and "sketchy AF."

"For months, we've been piecing together what they've done since they left the set," Chrysalis said. "I found it odd that their car was in New York City the day you escaped. And that there was an outgoing call on Mims's cell phone to Sara's number. Mims told us you'd used it but she didn't know who you had called."

"It seems like you have it all figured out," I said, in a last attempt to sow doubt. Of course Mims had told Chrysalis everything Kipps and I had done and said that day in her apartment. She hadn't kept even one of her promises to us.

"Sara and Charli think they can do whatever they want and say whatever they want, and they are mistaken," Chrysalis went on. "You're mistaken, Jess. I know everything about them. I have their address, their bank statements, scans of their fingerprints and their faces. I know what time they get up in the morning and what they like to order for dinner. Nothing gets past me. Nothing."

"They didn't have anything to do with what happened tonight," I tried.

"Enough." Chrysalis put up her hands. "I can't actually listen to this anymore. From now on, you are here on my terms. You do what I say. If I want you on camera, braiding Kristen's hair and being best friends with Tyler and having some saccharine conversation with your mother about the birds and the bees or some bullshit, then you do it, because that's what the show needs." She spoke slowly, enunciating each word like I was a toddler. "You do it, because we have Sara and Charli now, and they will be punished if you don't. Every time you do something stupid, they will feel the consequences. Do you understand? Does that make complete sense to you?"

Everything I wanted to say I couldn't, the words dammed up inside of me. Sara and Charli were out there, at LLP's mercy, and I couldn't reach them. There wasn't anything except this, the walled-in set, with its rules and its cameras and mics in every crevice and corner. I thought of Kipps and Reed sitting in the booth outside, waiting for me. They'd probably started to wonder what had happened. I was suddenly terrified they might try to find me.

"Right, fine," I said, but I could barely hear my own voice.

"Exactly," Chrysalis said, her eyes narrowing. "Now you're starting to get it. I know about the texting, or whatever that toy is you've been playing with, so you might as well give that over too."

"Texting?" I tried to play dumb.

"Please." She rolled her eyes. "Who do you think told you to come here? We already found the app in Sara's phone. We know she was contacting you."

She held out her hand, waiting. I pulled my purse to my hip, undoing the clasp, and it was already hard to remember which button was for what, every thought flooding in at once. I pressed the left one, holding it down as I passed the Tamagotchi to her, hoping that would clear any lingering messages. She glanced at it before tucking it into the front pocket of her blazer.

"And everything you think you saw tonight, everything you think you know—erase it from your memory. I don't want to hear anything about this night moving forward, especially on camera. Understand?"

There'd be no erasing it, no forgetting. But I had to pretend, at least until I figured out what to do with it all. I nodded. Chrysalis bent the chip between her thumb and pointer finger, the metal twisting apart to reveal a wiry panel inside. She flicked it onto the ground and it lay there, inches from my feet, useless now. Destroyed.

25

Three days later, Kipps and I were in his Land Rover, staring at the red light, the blinker keeping time like a metronome. Now that I knew about the self-driving cars inside the set, I noticed he never paid that much attention when he drove. His gaze sometimes stayed too long on the rearview mirror, or he'd shift into park a few seconds too late. There was a metaphor in it, I was sure. Something about not having control, or the road being mapped out for you, or maybe being a passenger in your own life. I might've puzzled through it, had I not felt like my rib cage was caving in on itself.

"Reed has been having a real tough time lately." Kipps glanced to the air-conditioning vent, where the camera was hidden, its glass eye staring out at us. "He hates leaving the house. The doctor said he's developed agoraphobia."

"Agoraphobia," I repeated, and it was all I could do not to laugh.

"They want him to do a digital detox, to kind of reset

or something. No Sega, no Nintendo 64. He can't even use the phone." Kipps didn't look at me as he said it, and the air in the car was stifling. I didn't need him to explain what that meant. Chrysalis and her team had raided Reed's room, confiscating anything and everything that he might be able to use to get back into their system. His iPhone, his iPad, his computer—all of it. They knew we weren't the ones who'd located the footage on the server, and now they'd neutralized Reed as a threat, confining him to his room for . . . how long? Weeks? Months?

He turned up the long driveway to school, passing the north gym and circling around the back, to the upperclassmen parking lot. By the time I'd emerged from the back of the diner on Friday night, Kipps and Reed were gone. Chrysalis led me past the empty booth, past the soggy onion rings and my untouched sandwich, and drove me all the way back to my house, depositing me there for the weekend. Kipps was silent except for a few cryptic texts that suggested they'd been interrogated by the producers as well. He had his own list of instructions to follow, the first being to pick me up for school today as if everything were normal.

As Kipps circled for a spot, we almost mowed over a pack of junior girls standing between two spaces, staring at a crowd that had formed around a red Miata. Kipps leaned on the horn but they didn't move.

"What's going on?" I asked, rolling down the window.

Jen Klein was beside them, her palm pressed to her mouth, like she had to physically hold it shut. She pointed at the car. The front hood was covered with shaving cream. Even though it was melting, I could still make out the word BITCH.

"It's Val's car," Jen finally managed. "She was in early for the National Honor Society meeting and when she came out . . . this was there."

Val emerged from the center of the crowd . . . only it wasn't the Val I'd met a few weeks before. Her cheeks were flushed and she was muttering to herself as she dug through the back seat of the convertible, pulling out a blue Swickley High hoodie. She used it to mop the foam off the hood. I knew it was fake. This was just a new storyline orchestrated by the producers about her confronting what everyone in school said or thought about her, but she'd leaned into it, her rage palpable.

"What are you all looking at?" she yelled at the students who stood there, gawking. "It isn't funny."

But the group just laughed. One kid doubled over, shouting, "Oh shit!" As Kipps and I pulled into a far spot, I could still hear Val asking who saw what, and swearing she'd find out who did it. She gave a speech explaining how the word *bitch* had been weaponized against women who were smart and assertive—which was true, but I still couldn't help but hate her.

"I'm sure this will be all anyone talks about this week." Kipps raised his eyebrows, and I could tell he got it too. This was Val's promotion to guest star.

I was unbuckling my seatbelt when someone knocked on the back window. Suddenly Kristen was there, sliding into the car behind me. She didn't speak until the door was shut tight behind her.

"Exciting news," she said, and she seemed more amped than when she'd placed in the Swickley talent night, after doing her impression of Vice Principal Vacca. "We want to incorporate even more voting into the show."

"You sure you want to talk about this now?" I asked, pointing to the dashboard, where I could still see the camera in the vent. "Here?"

"Oh, we can edit this all out." Kristen handed us each what looked like a clear plastic pill. "These are your ear-pieces. They're going to tell you the voting results as they come in. All day long, through the '90s Mixtape social media feeds, we're going to be asking the audience what they want to see. Where you should go, what you should eat, who you should talk to on the next episode."

"So we're, like, robots now," I said. "Right."

"Famous, well-paid robots," Kristen corrected with a smirk. "Anyway, you'll get cues throughout the day. Chrysalis said she stressed how important it was, that you actually follow the producers' instructions from now on."

She paused, and Kipps and I just let the silence settle between us. Kristen didn't seem aware of what had happened on Friday, but I couldn't be sure. It was nauseating, the idea that she might know what Chrysalis was doing and still be sitting here, smiling as she gave us directions.

"We got it, Kristen," I said, tucking the earpiece into my right ear.

"We want more engagement," she went on. "Get viewers invested. As messed up as it was, when they livestreamed your escape and had the voting going at the same time, those were some of our best numbers ever."

"I'm so glad," Kipps said, deadpan.

"That it?" I asked, turning back to her.

Her expression shifted, and she seemed a little lost now, making a big scene of finding the door handle. "Anyway, you'll hear from me soon. It'll be me in your ear."

If she was waiting for a response, we didn't give her one. The voting would just provide more data for them, better strategies to manipulate and control the audience, so that when they expanded into the VR experience it would be that much more profitable. It all seemed too obvious now, how everything was tied to money.

Kipps and I just sat there, staring out the windshield. I let my hand fall to the center console, folding it over his.

"You ready?" he asked after a while, but neither of us moved.

"No."

"Neither am I."

Then he leaned over and kissed me.

<hr />

Kipps was right, the whole school was speculating about who hated Val Holmes enough to deface her car, and who had access to it that morning, and why today, of all days? During second period Hannah Herlihy discovered an empty shaving cream can in the girls' bathroom, and that sent everyone spinning with new theories, mostly about Val flirting with Liz Woodward's boyfriend. It was infuriating that Val's betrayal had gotten her exactly what she'd wanted—more screen time, a lucrative guest star role. I should've been mad, but it was hard to feel anything when Kristen's voice was in my ear every twenty minutes.

"So we have something fun planned for band," she cooed as I walked past the art wing. Band was my first class with Tyler, and I just knew they'd make me say or do something humiliating. "They want you to play . . . the cymbals. Hilarious, right?"

"I don't know how to play the cymbals," I said through my teeth.

"That's why it's funny. You're great at the keyboard, but this will be, like, unexpected. Plus the cymbals are just silly. Like, who plays the cymbals?"

"Uh huh . . ." But Kristen cut out before I could say anything else.

There'd been five votes already, and I hadn't even made it to lunch. Some of it was stupid, like telling me to buy a Crystal Pepsi from the vending machine instead of my regular Snapple, but then she asked that I sit next to Chris Arnold during history and talk to him about his breakup with Amber last year. He'd gotten all teary-eyed, and gone on a breathless rant chronicling the ways he could've been a better boyfriend, and did I think she'd ever take him back? The whole thing had made me uncomfortable, especially since we'd only had one serious conversation before that, about Chris's fear of Teletubbies.

When I got to the band room I went straight to the closet, where I found the old cymbals in their foam bag. I immediately noticed the snare drum was missing, which meant Tyler was already here. That was part of the appeal, right? Me having no idea what I was doing while he confidently led the percussion section in songs I'd only been playing for a week?

"Jess, I can't find the sheet music for the cymbals . . ." Mr. Betts lingered in the doorway. He looked perpetually befuddled, his combover sticking up from his bald head. "You have good instincts, though. Why don't you just try your best? I'll cue you at key parts."

I'd always had a soft spot for Betts, mainly because he seemed like an underdog among the Swickley faculty. I'd once discovered him alone in his office, picking at a Tupperware of tuna salad, while everyone else was at the Homecoming pep rally. But now he seemed just as phony as Miss Baxter, or Mr. Lyle, or Chrysalis herself.

"Fine, whatever," I mumbled, before pushing past him into the room.

Tyler didn't even look at me as I set up in front of an empty music stand beside him. He turned his drumsticks between his fingers, spinning them around, occasionally rapping one on his thigh. When Mr. Betts finally raised his baton, I smashed the cymbals right next to Tyler's head.

"What the hell?" Tyler whined as he came in with the drum beat for the *Star Wars* theme. I smashed them again, louder this time, even though Mr. Betts hadn't cued me. The whole period went like that, me randomly banging the cymbals together whenever I felt like it, and Tyler becoming increasingly annoyed. I was putting them back into the instrument closet, feeling quite satisfied with myself, when

Kristen's voice was in my ear again.

"So don't hate me . . ." I could almost hear her wincing as she said it. "We just got results in for another vote."

"And . . . ?"

Jeff Tan was shoving his French horn onto an upper shelf. He turned, thinking I was talking to him, then said something under his breath.

"The audience wants you to ask Tyler to be friends with you again."

"What? Why?"

"I don't know, it's just a vote," she said. "Everyone loves a good reconciliation story. Tell him you miss him, that you want to start fresh. I don't know."

"Yeah, you don't know," I said, pulling the earpiece out and shoving it into my pocket. It was better to just do it now, rip off the Band-Aid. Say it and leave. It felt doubly shitty that it was Kristen, of all people, instructing me to apologize to her boyfriend for being a manipulative little fake.

"Tyler!" I said it way too loud. "Can we talk?"

"What's up?" He dropped his drum beside the wall, leaning against it as if he needed it to hold him up. He looked annoyed already, and I'd barely said anything to him.

"I just wanted to say . . ." I wasn't sure if I could get the words out. Because this wasn't Tyler, the friend I'd grown up with, making clover necklaces in our front yard. It was Roddy Perkins. The person who'd lied to me, and used me, and kept acting like I'd done something wrong by calling him out on it.

"I wish we were still friends," I managed. "Let's just . . . bury the hatchet, you know?"

"Bury the hatchet?" he repeated.

"Just . . . put everything behind us. We were never supposed to be together anyway."

That, at least, was true.

"I didn't do anything wrong, Jess," he said, indignant. "You were the one who left the set without any explanation. And what? You wanted me to wait around, pining after you?"

"That's not what I wanted at all." I could feel it, how far away we were from that day at his house, in the bathroom, when for a brief moment I thought maybe he would be on my side. That maybe at least one person had been looking out for me. "Let's just forget it, okay?"

"No. Not okay." The flute section pushed past us. They were debating about NYSSMA solos, and I had a pang of jealousy that none of them had to have this conversation, that none of them had to deal with Tyler. "I want an apology."

"You want an apology?" I felt heat behind my eyes, and I thought of all the times he'd lied to me, all the times he'd been the one to let me down, even if I hadn't known that's what he'd been doing.

"That's right."

"I'm sorry, Tyler. Okay?"

Then he gave me the smallest smile. He opened his arms, waiting for me to come to him, to step forward for a hug. And the worst part was . . . I did.

26

"It must be hard for you, now that Tyler and Kristen are together." Chrysalis tilted her head to one side. Even in that stupid curly wig and blazer, all I saw was the person who was trying to destroy Sara and Charli, who was keeping Kipps and me inside the set against our will. I despised her, even if I had to sit there and nod and pretend.

"It's whatever," I said.

I ran my hands along the tweed couch, digging my fingers into the foam. I never knew you could hate an office so much, with its booger-yellow walls and its chintzy wood furniture. The window was close enough to the cafeteria dumpsters that I could smell old fryer grease and curdling milk.

"You can talk to me, Jess."

She leaned forward and put her elbows on her knees, waiting.

"I'm fine, really," I said. "I'm with Kipps. Everything worked out."

It was the audience, of course, who had wanted me to go to see my guidance counselor instead of study hall with Kipps. Kristen hadn't specified what we'd be discussing, but they'd put a gold plaque on the desk engraved with the name Mrs. Marberry, and there were framed photos on the shelves now. Chrysalis and the extra who played fireman Ted. Another of a toddler with spaghetti all over their mouth. It was starting to feel like these meetings were going to be a regular thing, that there'd be no escaping her.

"Look . . . Jess . . ." She scrunched her face, as if she were in pain. "I'm going to break the fourth wall here and just discuss the news today. What's going on outside of the set."

"The news?"

"The news that's come out about Sara Flores. The girl who played your sister—"

"I know who Sara is."

"Did you know about her illegal activities inside the set? Did you suspect something was off about her? What about her mother, Charli?"

My insides felt hollowed out. I kept my palms against the sofa, pressing down, steadying them. I'd followed the story through the weekend, how they were questioning Sara in relation to a data breach—there was a mention of evidence they had but were not at liberty to share with the public. By Saturday night she'd talked to everyone she needed to talk to, though—both she and Charli had. They were home.

"Just tell me," I said. "What is it?"

"They were arrested." Chrysalis's lips twisted, trying to fight off a smile. "It seems like Sara stole bank account numbers from cast and crew inside the set. She was siphoning off money for months, maybe longer. Money from extras. They weren't making even half of her salary."

"That doesn't sound like Sara."

"I know. Everyone is shocked."

Chrysalis shook her head, but she wouldn't make eye contact. Instead she looked down at the floor, and I could see how pleased she was, how she was trying not to crack.

"There must've been a mistake." I was hyperconscious that this was all being filmed, that I might be the only person in the world defending Sara right now. I was one of a very few who knew the truth. "That's not who Sara is."

"Oh, Jess." Chrysalis folded her hands together. "I'm sorry. I can only imagine how hard this is to hear. But there was no mistake. It seems like they've only scratched the surface. They're only beginning to understand the scope of what she's done."

They're only beginning. It wasn't enough, that they'd already had her arrested. They'd keep going until they completely destroyed her life.

"Who's they?" My voice was unsteady.

"The police. I think the FBI might be involved at this point. I'm not sure," she said.

"Right."

"You sound skeptical." Chrysalis was daring me to do it, to just say the thing. She was trying to see how far she could push before I broke. "I assure you Jess . . . this is serious."

"I know it's serious," I said, and my eyes swelled, my vision clouding over. I wasn't going to cry in front of

Chrysalis—not now, not ever. "Can I go? I want to get back to study hall."

"That's right. To Kipps," she said, raising her brow. If it was a threat, I couldn't be sure. Everything she said felt menacing now. "Yes, you're free to go whenever."

I stood and grabbed my jacket and backpack, throwing it over my shoulder. I was almost out the door when Chrysalis stopped me. She framed herself in the camera beside the couch. One hand rested on her heart, and she gave me this pitying smile, her eyes awash with tears.

"Just know that I'm here for you, Jess," she said. "We all are."

27

When I got home that afternoon, Fuller was the only one who greeted me. My parents usually forced me to have dinner with them, partially out of habit and partially because it was another opportunity for them to be on camera and move their own storylines forward, or push their branded products. My mother was renovating a house on Kirkwood Lane and she'd been fighting with the contractor, and lately my dad had been using our dinners to discuss his online personal coaching seminars. But the kitchen was quiet. I called upstairs but no one answered.

They knew something had happened at the Fall Formal. I wasn't sure how much they suspected beyond the story of Mr. Henriquez passing out, and the ambulance, and having to cut the entire scene. My mom usually watched the night's episode in her office, jotting down how much screen time we'd gotten and which storylines Chrysalis had focused on, and she'd grown increasingly agitated after she saw what had aired Friday night. They'd scrapped everything about the formal and instead made it about Tyler and Kristen's budding romance. How Tyler had created his own dance in the meadow of Lynwood Park, complete with candles and roses and a stereo playing "Secret Garden," that cheesy Bruce Springsteen song from *Jerry Maguire*. She'd called me into her office, confused. "That was supposed to be you and Kipps," she had said. "You and Kipps are the leads of this show. What happened?"

Fuller was jumping on my legs and whining, so I grabbed his favorite ball and went through the French doors to the back of the house. I hadn't even thrown it across the grass when I heard an unfamiliar voice.

"Yes, that's right," a man said. "You're the sexiest gardener alive. A little to the left. Now over your shoulder. Yes, perfect. Yes."

As I rounded the side of the house my mother was standing in a string bikini and board shorts, watering the flowers with our garden hose. She kept changing positions, sometimes resting her hand on her hip, other times putting a high-heeled foot on one of the decorative rocks by the garden. A sandy-haired guy circled her with his camera, taking pictures, occasionally dropping down to one knee to get a better shot.

"Mom? What are you doing?" I asked.

I could tell she'd heard me, but she was mid-photo and never broke her smile. She put her thumb over the hose and sent a spray into the air, the water catching in the late afternoon light. A rainbow appeared and disappeared in an instant.

"Mom?" I repeated.

"Can I take just a minute?" she asked the guy, who was already looking at the images on his camera. "Just one minute."

She dropped the hose in the grass and walked toward me. Her hair was styled in perfect blond waves. Her blue board shorts were unbuttoned at the top and even though she looked like she was about to go swimming, she had on full makeup, including fake lashes. Her yellow hibiscus bikini looked brand-new.

"Jess . . . I'm kind of in the middle of something." She brushed her hair away from her face.

"Are you having a photo shoot right now? What is this?"

"It's for my social media," she said. "Your father and I talked about it, and we really have to distance ourselves from all this stuff with Sara and Charli. It's really bad, Jess."

"So you're distancing yourself by . . . posting bikini photos?"

Sara had explained thirst traps to me. It was really weird watching my mom make them.

"We're focusing on new content," she said. "Content to remind the *Stuck* audience that they know us. That they love us. That we're here for them, and we weren't the ones hacking into people's bank accounts."

"They don't know that Sara did that. They haven't proven—"

My mom held up her hand. "I can't hear that kind of talk. Especially not on camera. And you need to know that you cannot contact her. No texting, no calls. If she reaches out to you, you have to ignore it. I'm serious, Jess."

I rubbed my face with my hands, and it was a momentary relief, not having to look at her.

"I've scheduled a shoot for you this week," she said. "We'll do some family photos too."

"No way." I glanced past her to the photographer, who looked like someone's creepy uncle. "I'm not doing that."

"It's not like we have a real choice . . ." she said. "The ratings on '90s Mixtape are down. We're getting less and less airtime, and now this. We did not need this kind of scandal."

"Fine. Whatever," I said, not wanting to argue. "Where's Dad?"

My mom's expression shifted, and she nodded to the house next door.

"He's at Belinda Danforth's. We've been toying with a new storyline . . . something about him flirting with Belinda and—"

"You're pretending Dad is cheating on you?"

"Not quite," she said. "It's more for the drama. Will he, won't he? Is this a marriage in crisis? What will happen if—"

"I can't," I said, and I was already turning back toward the house. The day had been too much, and all of it rushed in at once—the meeting with Chrysalis, having to apologize to smug, self-righteous Tyler, just because the audience voted on it. I couldn't, on top of everything else, think about how desperate my parents were to hold on to this show, even if it meant losing me in the process.

Fuller followed me into the house and up the stairs. I hadn't even made it to my room and already I could feel the conversation with Mom catching up to me. I was hyperaware of the cameras in the perfume bottles, and the camera in the ceiling fan, and the camera in my VCR. I hit the mute button on the remote to turn them off, then dropped my mood ring and necklace onto my dresser, along with the earpiece Kristen had given me. Then I went straight into the closet and fell down into a pile of clothes Mims had left there. They didn't smell the way my clothes smelled, and nothing was where it had been. My favorite sweater was still missing and I couldn't find my plaid skirt and everything about this house and this place felt wrong.

"I can't do this anymore," I said, and I didn't even try to stop the tears when they came. "This is so messed up. So, so messed up."

I kept seeing my mom in that stupid skimpy bikini, prancing around our yard like it was a Victoria's Secret runway. My parents had always been superficial and annoying, but it was somehow so much worse now without Sara. There was no one to roll my eyes with. I couldn't just walk across the hall to vent. Instead I was stuck in a closet, ugly crying, trying to keep my whimpering low enough that the bedroom mics wouldn't pick it up.

At some point I grabbed an old Lilith Fair T-shirt and pressed it to my cheeks, trying to mop the tears off my face. Above me, there was a low, creaking sound. When I looked up the attic door in the ceiling was open a crack. I hadn't remembered it being like that when I walked in, but I couldn't be a hundred percent sure. I stared at it, waiting, and then it dropped another inch. I could see an iPhone aimed at me.

"Turn off the light."

It was just a whisper, but I recognized the voice, even if I couldn't say from where. Something about it was comforting, though, and before I'd made a conscious decision I'd flicked off the switch, sending myself into the inky dark.

When my eyes finally adjusted, she turned on the phone's flashlight, creating a perfect, twinkling star above. The attic door came down in front of me. Two feet, then two more. The wooden ladder descended, landing with a thud just inches from my feet.

I took the first step, then the next, unsure what was waiting for me.

28

As soon as I was up there, I could only see a few feet in front of the phone's flashlight.

"One sec," she said. "Did you take off your mic?"

"Yeah, it's off."

The attic door pulled up behind me, and I heard an automatic lock rotate, holding it in place. Her hand was all warmth, and as she tugged me forward I tried to see beyond the stacked cardboard boxes of Christmas ornaments and retired stuffed animals, plastic bins filled with old clothes and blankets. It wasn't until I caught a whiff of her vanilla skin cream that I realized who it was.

"Amber?"

"Shhhhh."

I wanted to be mad, but there wasn't anything left in me. My eyes were swollen and pink, and my throat hurt from being so upset for so long, the skin around my nose rubbed raw. How could I be pissed at Amber when Sara and Charli had been arrested for something they didn't do? When I was trapped inside the set, inside this life, taking orders from a faceless audience? All while my parents were downstairs, strategizing on how they might sell me out for another season?

When we got to the other side of the attic Amber used the flashlight to maneuver around several boxes, slipping through to a brick wall. If she hadn't stuck out her arm, I might've stepped right over the ledge and fallen into the hole beyond it.

"Is this . . . my chimney?"

My mom had put off fixing the flue for a decade, saying she didn't mind the fireplace being decorative. She'd packed it with birch logs and bought a wrought iron screen that made it feel cozy, even if we'd never once sat around it.

"Yeah," Amber said. "It's not actually broken. Never has been."

Amber went first. When she descended past the third rung she triggered a sensor, and the whole chimney lit up from within. The ladder dropped three stories, connecting to a tunnel beneath the house. As soon as we hit the cement floor I followed Amber around a bend and down a narrow corridor, my hand brushing against the cinder block wall. She didn't speak until we reached another set of stairs that emptied into a lounge with two leather couches.

"Where are we?" I asked, noticing the walls. They decorated the place with framed stills from previous seasons of the show. There was a photo of me when I was five, doing handstands at Maple Cove. Another from last year's pep rally, when the varsity soccer team hoisted Kipps onto their shoulders.

"A break lounge. But technically? Carol Pembroke's shed."

From the rectangular window I could see the plastic lounger where Carol sometimes lay in her one-piece, her skin slick with baby oil. Amber scrolled through something on her iPhone, then tucked it back in her knapsack, zipping the pocket shut.

"What do you want? I did everything Kristen asked me today."

"I'm not . . ." Amber rested her hands on my shoulders and it was weirdly comforting, being close to her again. "It's been torture, watching you hang out with Val Holmes for the past few weeks, like she's this really honest, upstanding person. She's beyond duplicitous. And she definitely wasn't the one who tried to help you that day in the lounge. It was me. I was the one who gave you the Tamagotchi."

It was almost like she'd said it too quickly, I had to keep repeating it to myself, puzzling through what she'd meant. If Amber had given me the Tamagotchi . . . she must've been helping Beyond1998. She was on our side.

"Wait . . . when? How?"

"When I was changing. I slipped it in your pocket as you were walking out."

"Why?" I must've said it too loud, because she brought her finger to her lips for me to be quiet. Then she double-checked the window.

"That day, in the locker room, when my phone fell . . ."

She leaned in closer, her voice almost a whisper. "I know there are all these theories online that I did it on purpose, or I was trying to warn you. I wish I could say that I was. But whatever, I'm glad it happened. Because you deserved to know. You always deserved to know, Jess."

"So you're part of Beyond1998 . . ."

"Now, yeah. I've been following the feed for the past few months. And I want to help them. I'm not the same person I was even a year ago—I see it now, Jess. After you left, it just felt so clear to me, that what we were doing was wrong. I went back through old episodes of the show and I could see how it was destroying you. The lies. Sara's illness. It was hard to watch."

I wanted to believe her, I did, but I had a sudden surge of anxiety. I'd just told her about Beyond1998, even if I hadn't explained exactly what it was. "How do I know you're even telling the truth?"

"I know what they did to Rae," she said. "How no one has heard from her since February. I know they basically bankrupted Arthur Von Appen and now they're going after Sara and Charli too. I know."

She pulled a folded note from her back pocket and pressed it into my hand. "I need you to get this to Reed. I just took a video of you before, in the closet—"

"You did what?"

I couldn't believe she'd just given me that whole story about being with Beyond1998, of wanting to help, right after secretly filming me.

"Please Jess, just listen to me," she said. "The audience

only sees what LLP wants them to see. We need to show them what's really going on with you behind the scenes. The voting is taking a toll on you, I know it is. And it's not going to stop until we make it stop. You're Chrysalis's puppet."

I unfolded the piece of paper in my hands. It had a specific date written on it—an upcoming Saturday. It also had a login for an AOL account and something about joining a chat room at a certain time.

"I want to release that video, and the ones you and Kipps filmed with Mims. The ones where you talk about how LLP doesn't own you and you don't want to come back to the show. But I have no idea how to do that without it being glaringly obvious it's me. Ever since Chrysalis found out about Sara and Charli, we've all been under a microscope. She's suspicious of all the producers now. With all the leaks, it's obvious certain LLP employees have been breaking their NDAs. I just . . . I need Reed's help. Isn't he, like, Mensa level or something?"

I'd already taken the note but now that I had it, I had no idea what to do. I just held it there between us. "Even if I could get this to him," I said. "He's like Rapunzel, locked away in his tower. They took his iPhone, his iPad, everything. He wouldn't be able to help you even if he wanted to."

"There's still one computer in the house," Amber corrected. "They have this ancient Mac in their den that's part of the set, but it's technically connected to LLP's network. He can get online that way and he still has access to the production and fandom chat rooms. It's part of this fake AOL software they've created. I can find him in there."

I slipped the note into my front pocket, holding my hand over it to keep it in place. I wasn't sure what the protocol was—if I was supposed to thank Amber or what. It felt like after everything that had happened between us, we were finally on more even footing.

"Did you hear about Friday night?" I asked.

"Wait . . . you were the ones who broke into the editing bay? Chrysalis mentioned something had happened, but I definitely didn't know you were part of that."

"We found all this footage," I said. "The last few minutes Rae was on camera. Chrysalis destroyed the chip before we could do anything with it."

Amber rubbed at her temples. "Listen, Jess. You need to protect yourself. You can't let Chrysalis and LLP control the narrative. You're at their mercy, especially now that they're using Sara and Charli to blackmail you. They can do anything to you and get away with it."

"I know," I said. "But what does that even mean? Control the narrative?"

"They gave you a phone. You're allowed to have it inside the set—it's in your contract. So use it. Create an Instagram feed, a Zing account, anything. Start posting different parts of your day. Update the audience on your life, so they know where you are at all times. Start livestreaming. Respond to your DMs. The more you talk directly to the audience the better. You need to keep that channel open . . . just in case. It's the only way to beat her, Jess."

"Right," I said, but the thought was overwhelming. Most of what I knew about social media was related to my parents, and the hours of videos I'd watched after leaving the set. My mom's rambling monologues, or how she sometimes took a selfie right out of the shower, her hair wet, the towel barely covering her boobs. Or my dad's "Five Minutes with Carter" segments, where he answered questions about his life and brand. I'd scrolled back months, and then years, to all the photos they'd posted of me without my permission. It was hard to think of social media as anything other than this horrible, exploitative thing.

"I better go. The tunnel branches off and circles back to an exit," Amber said, pointing to the stairs. "Wait a few minutes, then leave the way we came in. Close up the attic and just . . . try to go back to normal."

"What is normal anyway?" I joked.

"Good question."

Amber gave me a quick hug before she left. It was a relief, feeling like she was on my side, that she knew the truth. That even after working on the show for so many years, she saw LLP for who they really were. That she was as worried about Sara as I was.

I turned the note over in my pocket, wondering if it was too late to go to Kipps's house. There had to be a way to reach Reed.

29

I leaned back on the lounge chair, letting the sun warm my skin. Sometimes, when I closed my eyes, I pretended we were still in Maine. That Kipps and I were still on the beach, and Sara and Charli were at the house, and soon we'd cut over the dunes and through the woods to join them for dinner. I could almost hear Sara grumbling about my undercooked pasta. Charli would grab her phone and then we'd start debating what she should order, and we'd all get hangry, as Charli called it, because it took forever to actually agree on anything.

"We are maybe the worst pool people," Kipps said, but I still didn't open my eyes.

"Speak for yourself. I like how I pool."

It took two days before I made it to Kipps's house. I'd only ever seen the place in clips from the show, but it was even more ridiculous in person. An abstract, glass-block-ridden ode to the nineties, complete with elevator. Pale pink carpets lined every room, and they had a white baby grand player piano on the main floor, which spontaneously launched into renditions of "Can You Feel the Love Tonight" and "It's All Coming Back to Me Now." Nothing about it said Kipps Martin, but I guess with the exception of my room, nothing about my house said anything about me.

Kipps rolled onto his side and I finally turned to look at him. He was in his board shorts and a Swickley Soccer hoodie. I was wearing my Mets sweatshirt, even though it was seventy-five degrees outside. Despite voting that I make my parents breakfast in bed and have a "pool day" with Kipps, the audience had never specified that we needed to wear bathing suits.

"I honestly think no one wants to see me without my shirt," he said it so low I could barely hear him. "Which is fine by me."

"Their loss."

"Right?"

"They wouldn't be able to handle the hotness."

"Truth."

"Reed's definitely not coming down?" I asked.

I stared at the window above the den. It was weirdly easy to figure out which room was Reed's. Their parents had floral curtains. Kipps had a soccer ball decal on his window and two gold plastic trophies on the ledge. Reed's window had an old K'Nex set in it that he must've made years ago but never taken apart.

"Definitely not."

"Maybe I'll go up and say hi," I said, pushing my hands

into my sweatshirt pocket, and turning over the folded note that was there.

Kipps shook his head. "Ehhh . . . you're really not supposed to."

"Yeah, wouldn't want to upset anyone."

By anyone, I meant Chrysalis. Production had limited Reed's contact with everyone, and even though they hadn't specified that I couldn't talk to him, part of me expected alarms to go off as soon as I walked through the back gate. I'd thought about giving Kipps the note, but I'd have to explain it, and explaining it would mean implicating Amber, and I didn't want anyone else to be exposed because of me. It was bad enough they'd taken away all of Reed's electronics and started monitoring his time outside the house more closely.

My earpiece crackled, and I could tell Kipps heard it too, because his hand went to his temple, as if he had a headache.

"Another vote just came in," Kristen said, and she sounded excited. "The audience wants a double date."

Before I could process what was happening, she and Tyler bounded into Kipps's yard. Tyler was already shirtless, a beach towel slung over his shoulder. Kristen followed along behind him in her bikini and shorts, waving at us as she latched the gate.

"Bombs away!" Tyler yelled as he ran past. He ditched his towel and flip-flops on the grass and launched himself out over the deep end, already curled into a tight ball by the time he hit the water. Kristen stopped to peel off her shorts.

"What are you two doing? Get in," she said, pulling out

her ponytail so her hair fell down around her shoulders. She dipped her toe in. "It's warm."

As she moved her foot back and forth Tyler grabbed her leg, and she did a few awkward hops before crashing in beside him. When she got to the surface, they were both laughing. Then they started splashing, sending handfuls of water onto the lounge chairs. Kipps and I jumped up, trying to get as far away from them as possible.

"I don't have my bathing suit on," I lied. And I could already feel the afternoon turning, how grating it would be to have to endure both Kristen and Tyler for two whole hours, maybe more. What, were we supposed to strip down and play Marco Polo with them? Have float races and handstand contests like we did when we were younger?

"We should have a chicken fight," Tyler suggested to Kipps. "You and Jess versus me and Kristen."

"I'm good," Kipps stepped into the grass, his hands raised in surrender.

"You scared?" Tyler flicked his hair back, sending a spray of water toward us.

"We just don't feel like it," I said.

I knew we were supposed to at least try to have fun with them, but nothing about this was fun. Lately just looking at Tyler's face annoyed me. His features had somehow morphed into something strange . . . grotesque. I knew I was supposed to feel something about his ropey chest and biceps, but all I noticed was his spray tan. He hadn't picked the right shade and now his skin was just a few degrees away from Oompa Loompa orange.

"You can swim." I sat down on the edge of the pool, putting my legs in up to my shins. "We'll just hang out here. It's kind of cold, anyway."

"I'll show you cold," and then Tyler sprang forward, reaching out for me. Kristen threw herself over his shoulders but he'd already gotten my legs, and within seconds I slipped off the edge and was underwater. My hands immediately went to the note inside my front pocket, holding it there. When I came up for air my hair was in my face and the sweatshirt was heavy on my shoulders.

"Why do you have to be such an asshole?" I said, not caring what the scene was supposed to be, what I was supposed to say or do. "It's like you go out of your way to be annoying."

He looked momentarily stunned, but then he fixed his expression. "And you go out of your way to be a drama queen. It was a joke. Get over it."

"Jokes are supposed to be funny," I said, hoisting myself out of the pool. I just wanted to be free of my clothes. My sweatshirt felt like it weighed a thousand pounds. The hem was dripping, sending pool water streaming down my legs.

Kristen's and Tyler's towels were on the grass, but I felt like it might weaken my stance, using them when I was supposed to be pissed.

"There are more towels in the upstairs bathroom," Kipps said. "I can go get them."

"No, I'll do it," I said quickly. "I need to change anyway. I'll be back in a few."

Kipps's parents were supposedly at a PTA meeting, but I had to imagine that was more about getting us alone and less about their interest in the internal workings of Swickley High. I went straight to the upstairs bathroom and peeled off my clothes, leaving them hanging on the shower rod. Then I wrapped myself in the fluffiest towel I could find and sat down on the tub, trying to shake off the cold.

Two minutes, three tops. It wouldn't be long before it was suspect that I was still there. After Chrysalis's threats there was no way I could just knock on Reed's door and pretend like things were normal, that I was just popping in for a chat. They'd probably send the LLP security team over before I could get a full sentence out. They'd spend the rest of the day searching through Reed's room, just because I had set foot inside.

I checked the note. It was wet, but the ink hadn't run. It was folded into a square just smaller than my palm. I picked up a Pantene bottle, wondering if I could just hide it underneath, but it was too much of a risk that someone else might discover it first. Instead I went through the medicine cabinet, past old toothbrushes, sunscreen and bottles of AXE body spray. It was only then that I saw the coral pink container with the initials R.M. on the side.

It looked like a retainer case. When I opened it up it had two rows of clear plastic braces you snapped in. Reed must've been using them, hopefully enough that he'd find the note here. A minute passed, and another, and I made a big production of flushing the toilet, trying to give myself just a little more time to think.

It was a risk, but everything was a risk.

I tucked the note inside the case and snapped it shut.

30

My mom was superficial and had spent fifteen years lying to me, all to improve the ratings of a television show I never even knew I was on. She checked her makeup no fewer than twenty times a day—in the rearview mirror and with her iPhone camera and in the reflective panel in the microwave. She was wrong about almost everything, but she'd been right about social media. Her photographer had taken dozens of pictures of me and every time I posted one, my feed went crazy. Two posts in two days, and I'd gotten more than thirteen million followers. Whenever I checked, the number kept growing.

The latest photo was of me peeking out of the tree house window. He'd caught me mid-breeze, and my hair was blown back, my eyes squinting against the sun. I don't know if he'd photoshopped me or Facetuned me but the zit on my chin was gone, along with the mole above my eyebrow. Everything about me looked polished . . . perfect.

I lay back in bed, my thumb hovering over the button, until I finally worked up the courage to post it. My messages on Instagram had been going nonstop since I'd created an account, and I'd tried to keep up with them, but it was almost impossible. They'd picked up again and so had the comments on my other posts, mostly innocuous pictures of me on the tire swing in our backyard or poking my head out of the treehouse window. When I scrolled down I noticed one that said: *ARE U OKAY?? TELL US YOU'RE OKAY!* There was a snarky comment about the Delia's shift dress I was wearing, but the rest were a lot of the same.

This IS so messed up
I can't believe how upset she was
send us a sign ur ok
What is wrong with you people that you think this entertainment?!?
JESS FLYNN NEVER CRIES!! NEVER!!!

Some of the commenters had gone back and analyzed my first posts, trying to interpret if I was trying to tell them something, by standing in front of fire hydrant (*she needs help*, one commenter wrote. *she's sounding an alarm!!!*). Other comments were inundated with emojis, some I could translate, like a devil's face or a row of hearts. I had no idea what others meant. Someone named Crushzzzzez had posted three skulls and a butcher's knife, and I really hoped he hadn't meant it in a threatening way.

It wasn't until I went to the video feature that I saw what

everyone was responding to. Every other video was of me, sitting on the floor of my closet, crying into my Lilith Fair T-shirt. "This is messed up," I said. "So, so messed up." Then more sobbing. A graphic over it read SECRET FOOTAGE OF JESS FLYNN BREAKING DOWN AFTER DAYS OF AUDIENCE VOTING. Amber and Reed had managed to release the clips. They were everywhere.

Part of me was mortified that everyone was seeing me like this—vulnerable, exposed. But another part was relieved. Because Amber was right. It *had* worked. The entire internet felt sorry for me. My DMs were filled with fans asking if I was okay, or apologizing for their part in the voting. There were trolls, as Sara had described them, but other people were questioning LLP now. *No one talks about how screwed up it was that they faked your sister's death!! YOU WATCHED HER DIE!!* one person wrote. Another comment said, *That Chrysalis lady seems EVIL.* I was trying to read through them all when a text from my mom popped up.

9:39PM

In my office, now.

I felt nervous, but the good kind of nervous, like things were finally happening. Amber had been right about controlling the narrative. Now that I was online, and the audience had direct contact with me, I had a voice. Chrysalis didn't decide what happened on my feeds, and now that I had a presence there, it would be weird if suddenly . . . out of nowhere . . . I didn't.

When I got downstairs, the pantry door was open. I pushed the can to the right and the office door slid back. Both of my parents were there, leaning over my mom's desk, watching two screens at once.

"What is this?" my dad asked.

"When did this even happen? Who took this?" My mom held her phone up to me.

It was the same clip I'd seen four times already, with the text over it. She'd found it on Zing, and there were dozen more versions as she scrolled down, some with people green-screening themselves in to provide commentary. She kept scrolling, then showing me a new one, as if they were all equally disturbing.

"I don't know who took it," I said. "I was in my closet. I was upset."

"We're closing off that door," my dad said. He clutched the desk with both hands, as if it were holding him up. "We never should have let them make that an entry point. Now everyone thinks you're in some kind of distress. That we're keeping you here against your will."

"The worst part is those protestors are back." My mom pointed to one of the upper screens displaying an aerial shot of a crowd assembled outside the wall. They were holding signs and shouting, their arms raised in the air.

"Things were just getting back to normal," my dad said.

"Why were you so upset, Jess?" My mom launched it as an accusation, as if I had done something wrong. "Chrysalis is supposed to do a press conference now. It's a disaster. The *Stuck in the '90s* fandom is suddenly having all these feelings."

"We wouldn't want that," I said under my breath.

My dad straightened up, about to lay into me, but then Chrysalis's voice filled the office. She was standing outside the main gates of the set, wearing a chic black pantsuit, her hair slicked behind her ears. My parents were so quiet, so fixed on the screen, you would've thought it was a State of the Union address.

"I'm here because I saw the same video you saw," she started. "And I was equally disturbed. As I've said before, I love Jessica like a daughter. I, like you, hate seeing her in pain. It causes me pain." She looked down at her hands, probably trying to feign some kind of emotion, but when she raised her head her expression was still flat. "We're looking into this video, and the circumstances around how this happened, and starting immediately, the audience voting will stop. It was intended as a way to engage viewers, and the thought that it unintentionally harmed Jess . . . it's very upsetting. Obviously."

"She's such a liar," I said.

"Jessica," my mom said. "She's trying to help you."

"She's full of shit. Come on, you don't see how full of shit she is?"

But then I took in their blank expressions. I'd momentarily forgotten that they admired Chrysalis. They considered her their boss and collaborator and mentor. I'd once heard my mom refer to her as "a visionary" and "beyond talented." Normally I would've been furious at them all over again. Normally it would've eaten away at me. But now I just let out a long breath and tuned them out as they went on about not wanting to jeopardize our role on the show. My dad talked about respect and the life they'd given me, and then my mom did this whole melodramatic monologue about how Chrysalis truly cared about our family.

I just stood there, trying to keep what Amber had said in my mind. I had a social media following now. The audience was paying attention. People were worried about me and weren't afraid to speak up if anything seemed off.

There was only one way to beat Chrysalis, and I'd found it.

31

I didn't hear from Chrysalis until the next day, when the speaker in the gymnasium crackled and I was summoned to Mrs. Marberry's office. We were in the middle of a heated game of dodgeball, and my team was getting creamed. Amber and I were the only defense, and we'd spent the entire period darting back and forth, trying to land at least a few good blows. Jess Weinberg had horrible aim, and Bill Gorski just stood there, frozen, watching a giant welt bloom on his right arm.

Now I had to abandon Amber, and it all felt wrong. We were a team.

"Good luck," she said. I'd known her long enough I could tell she was nervous for me.

By the time I changed and made it to the other side of the school, there were only ten minutes left in the period. I passed Ben Taylor on my way into the guidance counselor's office, and instead of ignoring me like he usually did, he gave me this sad half smile.

"You good, Flynn?"

"For now."

Then he did the weirdest thing. He gave me a fist bump, as if I were one of his soccer bros. It seemed like everyone had seen the video of me losing it in a pile of sweaters, and now everyone was rethinking whether or not this whole enterprise was ethical, using someone's life as entertainment. Even Ben Taylor, king of public humiliations, was being nice to me.

"Jessica, I'm so glad you're here," Chrysalis said as I walked into the guidance counselor's office. She stood and hugged me, holding me for too long. "This just kills me. I hate that you're upset."

She made a big show of blotting her eyes with her knuckles, then gestured to the elegant woman sitting on the couch. "This is Dr. Dalal. I brought her here to talk to you. I have to apologize Jess, I thought you knew about all the resources available to the cast. I didn't know you were suffering. You never have to keep quiet about it."

Dr. Dalal wore a flowered dress that buttoned all the way down the front, her long black hair pulled back in a claw clip. "I'm a child and family psychologist," she said, reaching out her hand for me to take. "I've been practicing for almost twenty years now. Mrs. Marberry thought it might be good for us to talk at some point. Maybe not right this instant. But when you're ready."

Mrs. Marberry. There was something particularly heinous about Chrysalis using her sweet, caring guidance counselor alter ego after all the threats she'd leveled at me.

She watched me and Dr. Dalal, her hands folded beneath her chin in mock concern. Part of me liked seeing her so desperate—to prove she cared, to make me happy. I knew it was an act, but for the first time since I'd gotten inside the set, she wasn't demanding I say or do what she wanted. For the first time I felt like I had real control.

"Let me guess," I said. "Mrs. Marberry will be sitting in on every session."

Dr. Dalal glanced between us, unsure. "Is that a joke?"

"She monitors everything I do."

Then Chrysalis rushed forward, pulling her chair in close.

"Jess, that's just not true." In the curly wig, with no makeup, she actually looked like someone's mother, stricken with concern. "Why would you say that?"

"That's how I feel."

"Well, we're going to work on that."

I was hyperaware of the cameras around the room, hidden in the lamp and the psychology textbooks. Chrysalis might've set the scene to make her seem more sympathetic, but I had the ability to change that at every turn. There was only so much you could edit around.

"What do you think?" Dr. Dalal asked. "Would you be open to speaking with me at some point?"

"Off camera?"

"Of course off camera." It was possible she was just as good a liar as Chrysalis was, but she seemed sincere. She'd never once broke eye contact with me.

"That might help. Yeah."

Chrysalis pulled her chair in another inch, the point of our triangle. She kept shaking her head, her eyes filling with tears. "Jess, I just need you to know how sorry I am," she said. "I didn't know you were hurting. It was devastating for me, seeing that video. I think it was for the entire *Stuck* family."

"Right . . ." I couldn't hide the edge in my voice.

"I'm sorry, Jess. I don't know how else to say it," she tried, throwing up her hands. She glanced sideways at Dr. Dalal. "I'm sorry. Can you at least try to forgive me?"

It was so convincing. Had I been outside the set, watching on an iPhone, I probably would've loved Chrysalis right then—she seemed absolutely destroyed that she'd hurt me. But it was only for the cameras, and I was aware enough now to see that. So I raised my chin and focused on the glassy, domed lens in the bookshelf, sandwiched between two psychology textbooks. It was no bigger than a pencil eraser, but it was everything.

"I don't know . . ." I tried to seem removed, contemplative. "I'll have to think about it."

<hr />

When the bell rang, I didn't bother going to home ec. Now that I'd had a glimpse of 2037 the class felt especially archaic, watching Mrs. Landsby making a big show of sewing a button back on a shirt when tailoring kiosks could do the job in less than three minutes. She'd lost me last year when I had to keep an egg baby alive—mine had cracked along the bottom, oozing smelly stuff for a whole week. Landsby had lectured me as if it were a character defect, ignoring Biff Bunning, who had boiled his and ate it for breakfast.

The halls were full, and even the extras I didn't know smiled or waved when they passed. I cut across to the pink-tiled girls' bathroom, which felt especially dated now, in stark contrast to the all-gender restrooms outside the set. I slipped into one of the stalls and retrieved my phone from a hollowed-out copy of *Jane Eyre*. When I scrolled through it, my first instinct was still to text Sara. I kept wondering where she was, if she was okay, if she was scared. The articles I'd read said they were holding her in a juvenile detention center in southern Maine, but I couldn't find one on the maps or in any of my internet searches. It was as if she'd disappeared.

If I was going to locate her and keep her safe, I'd need help. And now that I was trapped inside, there was only one way to get it. In the past twenty-four hours, my following had grown from seventeen and a half million to nineteen million. I flipped the camera around, checking my light, because that was apparently something I did now. Then I made sure all of the stalls were empty before I started the livestream.

"Hi, it's me," I said, keeping my voice low. "I know all of you have been concerned since that video was released. I've rewatched it, and I'm equally disturbed that I was pushed so far. I just want to say that I'm okay. I'm going to be fine, but there are other people I care about who are suffering because of this show."

I adjusted the angle on the camera, making sure the fire alarm was framed on the wall behind me. The bright red box

had a lever with PULL DOWN printed on it. They were positioned all over the school, and freshman boys were always
setting them off on a dare, sending students streaming into
the hallways and out onto Swickley High's sprawling front
lawn.

It was one of the clues my followers were always turning
over. Did the fire hydrant in my second post mean anything?
What about the red turtleneck sweater I'd worn in my tenth
post? The truth was, they hadn't meant anything right then,
but that didn't mean they never could.

"Please, just keep an open mind. Don't believe everything
you hear. Don't assume anything. Think critically and do
your own research."

As soon as I switched off the livestream, I added hashtags,
even though I'd never used them before. I hoped that #be-
yond1998 would be noticeable but not completely obvious
to Chrysalis and the rest of the producers. I hid it among
#stuckinthe90s, #90smixtape, #ilovethe90s and a dozen oth-
ers. It was right there, hidden in plain sight, the ultimate
clue for anyone interested. Once more people found the
Beyond1998 feed and Sara's old threads, they'd see she'd
been homing in on LLP. She was as much a threat to LLP as
Arthur had been.

Within minutes it had thousands of views. Mentioning
Beyond1998 was a risk, but the audience needed to know
that there was a contingent of people who were against the
production company. Who had their own theories about why
Rae Lockwood and Arthur Von Appen and anyone else who
dared say anything about the company had gone missing or

been publicly maligned. Sara and Charli hadn't been arrested because they'd done anything illegal—they'd been arrested because they dared go against LLP.

It's a risk, I thought, *but people need to know.*

32

"Now?" I asked.

"Almost."

Kipps held tight to my hand, maneuvering me around something, then a few steps forward into the unknown. He shifted me to the left several inches, until I was standing in the exact right spot. I pressed the T-shirt to my eyes.

"I smell popcorn. We're at the Multiplex."

"No guesses. Come on."

He picked at the knotted fabric behind my head, letting the makeshift blindfold fall.

"I can look?"

"You can look."

The gates to Adventureland were open, the lock hanging down over the metal bar. The rides and games were in shadow. Giant stuffed pandas and fishbowls and a row of basketball hoops with cheap woven nets. On cue, the booth lights came on one by one, the attendants ready with darts and plastic water guns. The electric green and blue arrows on the Zipper, Adventureland's tallest ride, flashed against the night sky. Swickley's amusement park was notorious for blasting Z100 so loud you couldn't talk if you were standing directly in front of a speaker. But now the whole place was quiet. Romantic.

"It's just for us? How'd you do this?"

"Turns out there are some advantages to being one of a dozen people that actually live inside the set."

"Adventureland, but without all the lines or the cliques of St. Mary's girls."

It was magic, the way the whole place glowed. The tinkling sounds of carnival games filled the air. The carousel took a long, slow lap, and it was like a scene inside a snow globe, suspended in time, waiting just for us.

He grabbed my hand and pulled me farther inside, past the metal swings I hadn't been on since I was a kid, and the bumper boats, which were kind of gross, floating in murky yellow water that stained your clothes.

The thing I couldn't say, the thing I couldn't tell him right then, was that he'd known what I'd needed, and that was its own miraculous thing. Since I'd livestreamed about LLP there were too many comments and DMs and YouTube videos to respond to. Some audience members had found the Beyond1998 site and now extras were writing in with stories about how they'd been fired for the smallest things, like asking for a longer lunch break or a day off. There were names that kept appearing, other extras or LLP employees who'd been punished over the years. As hopeful as it was to see the perception of LLP shifting, we were still inside the set, still waiting to hear anything definitive about Sara or Charli. We didn't know if they had a court date, or the full extent of the charges against them. Things had yet to shift in our favor and Chrysalis was still in control, just like she'd always been. Still tracking our every move.

My parents had been livid about my cryptic livestream, but I'd known that was going to happen. Being with Kipps was a brief respite from the pressure. We had this night, and we went to the Tunnel of Love and made out for the whole five-minute ride, because it was dark and we knew we could. I'd never been inside before and it felt like Kipps and I were drifting in space, the walls closing in around us as animatronic cupids flew above. We were sucked against the walls of the Gravitron. Kipps tried to lift his head to look at me but that only made it worse, and he slammed back into the padding. We ate cotton candy on the swings and I won a giant parrot in the ring toss game and gave it to Kipps, because I couldn't stand watching him try for the twelfth time. Then Kipps insisted on going on the Zipper.

Lately his mic had been in his watch. He fumbled with the leather strap and then dumped it in one of the lockers by the attendant, along with his hat. I tossed in my purse and mood ring and suddenly we were free, unencumbered as we walked to the metal cages.

"How you two doing?" The attendant was a fifteen-year-old boy with braces and spiky black hair. His polo had ADVENTURELAND and CLIFF embroidered onto the chest.

"We are . . . *divine*." Kipps made a big show of the word.

I'd once told him he was sometimes Weird For No Reason, and we'd started abbreviating it, our own shorthand joke.

"WFNR," I said, then turned back to Cliff. "We're good. Considering."

He nodded as if he knew what I meant, then opened the latch on the third cage.

"No—we'll take this one." Kipps moved down to the fifth cage.

The boy seemed confused. He didn't have an earpiece and he turned back, scanning the rest of Adventureland for a producer who never appeared. After a beat he just walked down to the fifth cage and opened it for us, then secured the lap bar and metal door. Kipps didn't say anything until Cliff was back in front of the controls, the ride purring to a start.

"Did you ever notice you've only ever been in the third one?" Kipps asked. "The third one, every single time. It's the only cage that has cameras and mics."

"That would be an odd thing to keep track of."

The lap bar pressed against our hips, pinning us to the seat. The cage rocked back and forth. I was about to ask Kipps why exactly we had to shed our mics for this particular ride but then we whipped forward, spinning out and up.

I was screaming. Kipps was screaming. It was different somehow, being here with him. I'd only ever ridden with Amber and Kristen. Back then I was letting go of something I had always felt but could never articulate, and I screamed for Sara and my parents and for the inescapable weirdness of Swickley, where I was always on the outside of its inside joke. But here, now, it was just . . . kind of thrilling. Fun.

I grabbed Kipps's hand and squeezed tight.

The ride threw us around. The cage flipped over, then spun out, the Spice Girls blasting over the sounds of metal clanking against metal. When we reached the top, the cages lined up, each one almost completely vertical. The ride paused and prepared to reverse direction.

"This is it." Kipps shifted, looking out the back. "We have ten seconds. Don't miss it."

I turned to see what he saw. I wasn't sure what to look for at first, but then it was clear: if you tilted your head you could see all the way to the other side of the set and beyond the wall. The outside world was a hundred times as populated as Swickley, a current of headlights streaming past, houses in every direction, and a cluster of towers behind them. The crowd of protestors had grown and was now hundreds strong.

"I came here almost every day the year before we left," Kipps said. "Just to remind myself it was still out there. That there was more than this."

One side of his face was in shadow, the other glowing red and blue from the flashing lights. I wanted to hug him but I couldn't, so I just squeezed his hand tighter.

"It was always there," I said.

"We're going to be okay, I know we are. I can feel things tipping in our favor."

"People are starting to think about the show differently," I said. "They're starting to get it. We just have to wait it out, then we'll go. We can go back to Maine."

He just shrugged, and it broke me a little, thinking of him

alone on the ride, living for this brief reminder. With the way the cage was assembled, it was only a sliver, a seven-inch gap you could peer through. It was nothing and everything.

The ride started back again, flipping us around, and I felt like I might cry. I hadn't even gotten the chance to kiss him.

33

The girl at the strength test was heckling me. We'd spent more than three hours inside Adventureland, riding rides, shooting water guns at metal targets, and throwing darts at balloons. Now our arms were loaded with extra tickets, a giant stuffed parrot, a stuffed monkey, and an off-brand Hello Kitty doll. Kipps had won a goldfish in a tiny plastic bowl, and he was already worried he wouldn't be able to keep it alive. We'd almost made it to the parking lot. The last thing we wanted to do was smash a six-foot mallet into the ground.

"Come on, win your guy a prize!" The girl had purple hair and a septum ring.

"We're okay."

"You afraid you're not strong enough? You don't have what it takes?"

The prize wall behind her was covered with tie-dyed teddy bears. She stared me down, giving me this intense look that made me think she knew me, which I guess she did. Normally I would've ignored her, but something about it felt off.

"Fine . . . I'll try."

"Challenge accepted." Kipps laughed.

I unloaded the stuffed animals into his arms. When the girl handed me the mallet it weighed three times as much as I was expecting, and I lurched forward under its weight, nearly dropping it. I only managed to throw it down once, and I hit the edge of the metal platform before smashing it into the ground.

"You almost broke my foot," Kipps said.

"You're going to get me fired . . ." The girl smirked, then gestured for me to give the hammer back. "But I'll give you a consolation prize. How about one of these small guys?"

She pulled one of the tiniest teddy bears down from the wall and handed it to me. It had a creepy smile, its black eyes frozen in mock surprise. I'd rather have chosen it myself, just to be sure she wasn't passing off a secret camera or mic, but I made a mental note to check it before bringing it into the house.

"Make sure you take good care of him," she called after us. "He's special."

I wasn't sure what she was getting at. The thing looked like a Grateful Dead dancing bear knock-off—just a little too plump, and without the jester collar.

"Kiss me, out of the bearded barley." The music swelled around us, so loud I could feel it in my chest. "Nightly, beside the green, green grass . . ."

"I've always liked *Stuck*'s personalized soundtracks."

Kipps hoisted the parrot over his shoulder. "It's a nice touch."

We held hands as we walked out of the main gate. Kipps's car was the only one in the parking lot. We climbed in and Kipps balanced the plastic goldfish bowl in one of the cup holders. We hadn't named the fish yet, but we were leaning toward Derek.

"Back to life, back to reality . . ." Kipps sang in the most miserable voice. Then he pulled out of the lot, taking a wide turn onto Uniondale Turnpike. I immediately started playing with the seam in the teddy bear's back, feeling for anything inside the stuffing. I picked at the thread, tugging at it, hoping it might break.

"This isn't reality. This is like . . . some bizarre simulation."

"A simulation where our parents are pissed at us all the time. And we're being blackmailed. And our only contact with the outside world is through social media."

"Totally normal."

"Totally."

As we pulled up to the red light by the 7-Eleven, it blinked three times, then switched to yellow, then red again. At first I thought I'd imagined it but then it repeated the pattern, eventually landing on red and staying there for a full minute.

"Are you seeing this?" Kipps leaned forward to get a better view.

"It's having a meltdown." I looked down the street but there were no other cars in either direction. "Are they manually controlled?"

"I have no idea."

We stayed there, waiting, and I half expected Kipps to

just put the car into drive, but it was another minute before the light turned green and we were moving again. He seemed relieved, which was a relief to me, like watching the flight attendant on an especially turbulent flight. *Everything is okay. We're okay.*

"A glitch. Weird," he finally said.

The main drag of Uniondale Turnpike was deserted. I'd managed to poke a hole in the back of the teddy bear. I kept it faceup, rooting around inside with my fingers, looking for a camera or a mic, but I couldn't feel anything. We were about to reach the intersection with the Swickley Mall and Blockbuster, when I flipped the stuffed animal over and noticed the writing across its back.

Printed in tiny block letters was a message:

DO NOT GET IN THE CAR.
THEY'RE GOING TO KILL YOU.

I looked up at the red light several yards in front of us. The buildings on either side were all closed, their windows dark. The UN in the LAUNDRYMAT sign had gone out.

"Kipps, I need you to pull over," I said, trying to keep my voice calm. "I don't feel well. It must've been the cotton candy."

"Yeah, of course." Kipps scanned the dashboard, eventually grabbing hold of the cigarette lighter. He tugged on it but nothing happened. "I just have to . . ."

He yanked it harder, pulling it out, but it still didn't do

anything.

"What is that?"

"It's supposed to override the autopilot," he said. "Like a fail-safe. It's supposed to let me drive the car but it's not working."

"This is bad."

"It'll just route us to your house. It's fine." He fumbled around in the back seat. "Let me find you something in case you yack."

"No, Kipps, we have to get out of the car. Now."

I passed him the bear, not caring if one of the cameras saw the writing.

He was still reading it when we blew through the intersection. He tried to turn the wheel, then he tried to pull the parking brake, but the car didn't respond. The last thing I saw was his face, white in the glow of the truck's headlights.

34

The truck smashed into the back half of Kipps's Land Rover, sending us spinning out across the intersection. My body was pulled in one direction, then another, and we didn't stop until we rammed into the curb, sending the car pitching to the side.

For a long while, I could only hear the sound of my breaths. Two of the windows had broken and glass shards were caught in my hair. They settled in the folds of my jacket like tiny, twinkling jewels. The empty fishbowl rolled around Kipps's feet. Beside it, the fish writhed back and forth, desperate for water.

There was smoke and the smell of burnt rubber. The whine of twisting metal. Before I could think, I reached out, feeling for Kipps's hand.

It was only when I tried to talk that I realized I was bleeding. My lip and nose were already swelling, the skin fiery to the touch. "My face."

Kipps seemed dazed. He brought his fingers to his forehead, wincing as he inspected a cut just above his brow. The hood of the Land Rover looked completely normal, but when I turned around the entire back of the car was a mess of metal, and my seat was twisted sideways from the impact. The truck had missed me by two feet, if that.

"They're trying to kill us." I tried to unbuckle my seatbelt as I said it, but it was caught on a bent piece of the frame, and I had to duck to free myself. "We need to get out of here, Kipps." I grabbed his arm, trying to shake him into action. "We need to move, now."

I felt around my feet for my purse. My iPhone was zipped into the lining but my hands were shaking so badly I could barely get it out. As soon as I had it I tried to open Instagram and start a livestream, but I kept hitting the wrong buttons. The car was dark, and it took me forever to figure out how to get the light working, and then it was finally on. I looked worse than I felt, my cheekbone swollen, my hair a sticky mess of blood. I was sure I'd broken bones in my face.

"For anyone listening," I said, "Kipps and I are inside the set near the Swickley Mall. LLP has come after us."

I panned around the inside of the car, trying to show the destruction. Kipps had managed to get his seatbelt off. He was beneath the steering wheel, trying to save the fish. He put it back in the little plastic bowl but there was no water. It was dying and he was fumbling around, and neither of us could do anything to help.

"They're trying to kill us. Chrysalis is trying to kill us," I said, but even after all I knew about them it was hard to believe it was happening. "We need help."

I'd just tried to post it when someone reached through the broken window and grabbed the phone out of my hand. Chrysalis was standing right beside the car. She turned the phone off and then threw it down onto the pavement. Behind her, Melvin from the diner stepped out of his wood-paneled truck. Everything from the headlights to the windshield was pulverized, smoke trailing up in a long, black plume.

"What happened?" he said, stumbling forward as if he were drunk.

"We already have the crash footage," Chrysalis yelled. "You can stop, Melvin."

He straightened, suddenly sober. Then he studied the car, and me, trying to figure out if he'd done what he was supposed to.

When Chrysalis looked at me there was nothing behind her expression. It was as if she'd simply registered we were still alive, and that was bad, and now she had to carry out the next steps herself. She reached for my door handle but it was stuck. I crawled over the center console, pushing Kipps out. He finally saw Chrysalis and dropped the fishbowl.

"I need cameras paused. Everything erased from 9:56 on. And I want all available security teams to Uniondale and Jericho." She pressed her earpiece as she spoke. "Now."

As Chrysalis circled the car I grabbed Kipps's arm, tugging him toward the mall. It was closed, but the building would at least provide cover. If we could just get there, we'd have more places to hide.

Kipps was moving at half his normal pace, and he held

on to his head like it was throbbing. "Oh shit," he mumbled, and I saw it at the same time he did. Two Swickley Alarms cars rounded the corner and were blasting toward the intersection. We ran faster, going around the back of the building to where the dumpsters were. Various metal doors were labeled AEROPOSTALE and CONTEMPO CASUALS and GADGETS AND GIZMOS. I tried them all, becoming more desperate with each one. They were all locked.

The cars rounded the corner. The first one sped down the alley, directly toward us, trying to run us over. It would've managed to had I not pulled Kipps behind a dumpster. It went to the far end of the parking lot and flipped a U-turn, coming back for a second try.

There was only one public entrance to the mall—a set of glass doors several yards away that led to the back parking lot. I pointed to it, then grabbed a stray rock that was lying by a second dumpster. I ran as fast as I could and hurled it through the glass, smashing the bottom pane. An alarm blared. The car had completed its turn and was coming back now, swiping the side of the building as it aimed for us. We knelt down and climbed through the half-broken door. I pushed Kipps through first and all I could see was the car's fender coming toward me, the headlights blinding as I slipped inside.

The car rushed past, skidding to a stop somewhere behind me.

"Go, go," I said, but as soon as we were inside it was clear there wasn't anywhere to go. The alarm was even louder now, echoing off the tile interior. Every store had a metal grate pulled down in front of it, effectively sealing it off from the main concourse. We moved through methodically, checking the bathroom doors, but even they were locked. "We're trapped," I finally admitted.

Two of the LLP security team came through the broken door and were now right behind us. It was George, the same stocky guy who'd taken Kipps on the beach in Maine, and a middle-aged bald man I'd never seen before. They each had a long, black baton in their hand.

Kipps and I ran toward the main entrance, but when we got there the glass doors were chained shut. The closest trash can was attached to the floor. We didn't have anything to break through to the other side. The men stalked forward, spreading out behind us, and suddenly there was nowhere to go.

When I tried the door of Wicks 'N' Sticks, it was locked. Across from us, a metal grate was pulled down in front of the Pretzel Time counter, but I didn't see a deadbolt on it. I grabbed Kipps's hand and we ran for it. As soon as I reached the grate I yanked it up and it gave just a few feet. We slid underneath like we were in an Indiana Jones movie.

The security team tried to follow, but they were bigger and thicker than us, and they had to pull it all the way up to get through. It was just the lead we needed. We darted around the counter and into the back, but instead of a kitchen we were in a bare room, empty except for a single fridge and microwave. I slammed the door behind us and hoped it would give us more time. The far wall had an emergency exit, but I had no idea where it led to. When I pushed on the metal bar it gave, spitting us out on the north end of the mall.

The night air was cool against my skin. Kipps actually smiled as he fell back against the door, his face all relief. Then we turned and saw the parking lot. There were six Swickley Alarms cars in front of the main entrance. At least a dozen men and women in black polos were coming toward us. Occasionally they'd touch their ear, or their lips would move slightly, and I knew instantly what that meant.

They were listening to Chrysalis's directions.

35

"Just enough so it can still look like it was part of the accident," Chrysalis directed. She positioned herself behind one of the vehicles, watching the scene from a distance. "We're keeping the car crash storyline. Poor Melvin gets drunk after his night shift. Kills two innocents."

Kipps and I retreated, trying to get back inside the emergency exit, but the two men who'd followed us into the mall were now on their way out. I didn't know what else to do so I pulled Kipps against the side of the building. We held our hands up, shielding our faces, hoping it would provide some kind of protection. I kept waiting, bracing myself for what might happen next.

When we looked up, Chrysalis and the LLP security team had turned around, back toward the intersection. I heard it before I understood what it was. A scatter of random voices. Then a silhouette appeared, holding a sign, and then another. Three people climbed over the fence behind the Blockbuster and cut across the street.

"Where's Len?" Chrysalis scanned the security team. "You were on the south side. How are they getting in?"

A guy with a goatee shrugged. "I didn't notice anything."

"Shit, look!" A girl's voice split the air. A small group had reached the crumpled Land Rover. "She was telling the truth. Jess! Jess! Kipps!"

One of the security team yanked his zip ties from his belt and came at us, grabbing Kipps's wrist. But he paused when another group turned a corner. There were sixty or seventy more people now, and a few had their iPhones out, the flashlights twinkling in the dark. I thought I saw Amber and Reed in front of the crowd, but from so far away I couldn't be sure.

Chrysalis was the first to climb into one of the Swickley Alarms cars. Melvin was tucked in the back seat, watching the scene unfold through the window. The rest of the security team seemed frozen, unsure what to do without a direct order.

"Get them in the car and clear out. Before these people get any closer." Chrysalis banged her hands on the dashboard in frustration, and the driver finally entered something into the console. "Regroup at the Chateau."

The guy named Len turned toward us, but Kipps and I were already moving. We cut back across the lot and into the street. It took a minute for the security team to get in their cars and circle around, and by the time they did we were out in the open, in front of everyone. I waved both my arms above my head, hoping it would be obvious it was us.

There must've been two hundred of them. More were still appearing at the edges of the intersection. As the security team pulled away the crowd scattered, taking photos and video of the Land Rover and the swarm of Swickley Alarms cars as they retreated down the turnpike. It was only then that Amber broke out in front, running toward me.

She pulled me into the tightest hug. "I was so worried."

I noticed a boy with chin-length hair pass us, then circle the smoking car. He had a nose ring and leather jacket on. It wasn't Reed.

"We have to get out of here," Amber said. "We have a small window. They've probably already sent security to your houses. One of our Beyond contacts was supposed to get Fuller."

"Where's my brother?" Kipps scanned the crowd behind her.

"He was supposed to meet us here, but I don't see him," she said.

"Kiki Wilder! I need a selfie with you!" a girl in silver high-tops yelled. It took me a second to remember that that was Amber's real name. "Let's get one selfie by the wreckage?"

Amber grabbed both of us and started toward the Blockbuster parking lot. I doubled my pace, keeping my head down. I'd forgotten I was bleeding, but the sleeve of my jacket was stained, a dark red smear that went up my forearm. We'd already started climbing the fence when I noticed Kipps wasn't beside me anymore.

"Kipps, you're great but you have to move your ass," Amber said. "Seriously. I'm not going to get caught because of you."

I was clinging to the side of the fence, my toes wedged on a narrow slat. "Come on. We'll meet Reed outside the set."

"I can't."

I turned, watching Kipps as he looked from the Land Rover back to us. He still had his hand on the side of his head. At some point his flannel had ripped, exposing his arm, which was scraped raw.

"What do you mean you can't?" I said, jumping down. "Kipps, Chrysalis just tried to kill us. She's going to do it again. You're not safe. You have to come."

Kipps still didn't move.

"Amber, go," I said. "I'll meet you outside the wall."

"You have to leave through the exit in the Paulsens' basement. It's not going to be open much longer," she said.

She brought her hand to her neck, and I didn't know what she was doing at first, but then I realized she still had the BFF necklace on. She pinched it between her fingers, and for the first time I was sad that I didn't have mine. It was starting to feel important, this tangible link between us, so that no matter what happened after this we'd be connected. We'd come so far to get here, and we just needed to go a little farther. I hated the idea of not walking out of the set together. All of us.

"Hurry," she said.

"I will. Promise."

She nodded before climbing down the other side of the fence.

When I turned back to Kipps he had his phone out,

but every time he tried Reed those few high pitched beeps rang out, announcing the number had been disconnected. "There's no way to even reach him. He must've gotten stuck somewhere. We can't just leave him."

"But we don't know where he is. He could already be on his way out."

We scanned the crowd that had assembled in the intersection, but from where we were standing it was hard to make out anyone's face. Everyone looked the same.

"I don't want to leave him either," I said. "But if we don't go now we might not get another chance. It's not safe anymore, Kipps." I grabbed Kipps's arm and tugged. I didn't realize I was crying until I was, and then I could barely get the rest of the words out. "It's not safe."

"I'm not even eighteen, Jess," he said. "I'm still under that contract."

"Well, I'm pretty sure you can break it. There must be some clause that if the executive producer tries to kill you, you can get out of it."

I thought that had done it, that I'd gotten through to him. But instead he stepped back, his eyes awash with tears. Behind him the crowd was only growing, and multiple groups had started livestreaming in front of the Blockbuster. A dozen twentysomethings were taking selfies with the smashed Land Rover. I kept waiting to hear the squeal of the Swickley Alarms cars. They were going to come back, it was only a matter of when.

"I can't go without him," he said.

"Then we'll pass your house first, before we leave. We

just have to be careful."

"No, Jess. You go—seriously. Go."

I might've tried to argue, but I could tell he'd already made up his mind. He kept glancing behind him, to Old Hartford Road, which led back to the other side of town. If he left now he could get to his house in ten minutes. If Reed was there, and that was still an *if*, he could get him and still get out in time. If everything worked out, we'd meet up outside the wall. *If.*

"I'm going to find Reed," he finally said. "I can't leave him again."

Then he grabbed me and pulled me into a hug, and I don't remember what exactly he said, or what I said, or the sounds of the alarms blaring somewhere outside of us. All I know is he was there, and for that one last moment, we were close.

36

As soon as I got to the other side of the fence panic set in.
I was in someone's backyard, but I didn't recognize it, or
the moldy plastic slide sitting in the corner. I didn't remember ever being on this street, in this part of Swickley. Every
house looked the same.

I tried to slow my breaths but my lungs were tight and I
couldn't get enough air. My shock had worn off, my face and
arm now throbbing with a fiery pain. Sirens sounded behind
me. The Swickley Alarms cars had a specific, high-pitched
wail, and they mixed with the *whoop whoop* of police cars,
all rushing closer to the center of the set.

Amber had said the exit was in the Paulsens' basement. I
had nodded, nodded like an idiot, as if I knew exactly where
that was. I'd only ever crossed under the wall two times.
Through the tunnel below the main entrance and down the
staircase in the maple tree, that day when Kipps and I had escaped. It already felt wrong, that we were apart. That I'd left

Amber and Kipps and Reed and we were all doing this alone.

I crossed the lawn, which had been thrown into darkness except for a single lamppost that shone down from the Blockbuster parking lot. When I got through the side gate and stepped out into the middle of the street I still didn't know where I was. The whole block was empty, quiet, every window an inky black. I'd only seen the town like this in the days after the tornado, and after Hurricane Ainsley, which I was starting to believe had been real.

It wasn't easy, orienting myself through the pain. Part of me just wanted to lie down. I tried to think about the intersection behind me—the corner near the Swickley Mall. We'd been driving north, into the residential streets, when we'd been struck by Melvin's car. I figured I couldn't be more than a half mile away from the far side of the wall. I tucked my arm close to my body, holding it there to lessen the pain. As soon as I crossed through another yard, to the next street over, the houses seemed more familiar. At least I thought they did. I was making my way to the corner when every light in the entire set switched on.

Every streetlamp and window was suddenly lit, exposing the empty insides of each house. From where I was standing I could see the living room across from me. The window was dressed with a single sheer curtain, but there was a plastic folding table and chair beyond it, scattered with assorted makeup and brushes. It was eerie, realizing how alone we'd been inside the set. Swickley had always been described as a "sleepy town" but it was hollow, empty. Here and now, I could suddenly see it for what it was.

"Oh my god, I can't believe this." A woman's voice carried down the street. "Oh my god. I really cannot believe we're actually inside."

She ducked under a clothesline and was running toward me, two other women in tow. They looked like they were in their twenties or thirties. One, a redhead, was holding a rolled-up sign that said something about THE TRUTH. Another was filming everything with her phone. They must not have seen me, standing beside the porch, because they'd nearly passed when I called out to them.

"It sounds like Chrysalis's security team is on its way," I said, the sirens somewhere behind me. "They called the police too. You should turn back."

"Jess Flynn?" The redhead squinted in the streetlight.

"Which way did you come from?" I asked. "Is there an exit over there?"

"Yeah . . . the bright blue house," the girl with the phone said. "Two blocks over."

She spun around, tracing a circle with her phone, catching the set from every angle. She stopped on me, lingering for a few seconds too long, and I ducked my head as I ran past, to the yard they'd just come through. The last thing I needed was for LLP to see me on a livestream or in some Instagram post and realize where I was.

I moved faster, cutting through the dense trees behind another split-level house. It wasn't until I reached the next street that I realized where I was. Tyler's place stood behind me. The Paulsens must've been his neighbors. The few times I'd been over there I'd seen an elderly man trimming the rose bushes in the front yard.

A half dozen people ran up the Paulsens' basement stairs and out into the street, barely noticing me as they dispersed, heading toward the Swickley Mall. A few had their phones out but others were staring up at the set, barely moving as they took in the neighborhood. From somewhere behind me I heard a man's voice over a megaphone. "You are trespassing," it said. "If you do not vacate the property you will be arrested."

Still, no one changed course. When I reached the stairs there were still more people filing out, enough that I had to stand and wait my turn. I stood right beside the door, out of view, hoping no one would notice me as they passed. It took a few minutes before I managed to get inside, the cold tunnel a relief.

With each step I felt more confident. I was getting closer. I was going to make it out. I let my left hand drag against the concrete wall, my right arm tucked close to my side. The pain had momentarily subsided, my body alive as I neared the exit. I climbed the stairs slowly and stepped out into the open air. The dirt field was flooded with light.

Drones swarmed overhead. They all had different logos on them. As one dipped down, like a low-flying bird, I saw that NEWS 11 was printed on its underside. Another was labeled COUCH COMMENTATORS, after two women who had spun a YouTube show out of drinking rosé and talking shit on all of *Stuck*'s characters. The drones flitted this way and that, filming everything just beyond the wall.

"It's Jess Flynn!" someone yelled, and everything in me

wanted to disappear.

"Jess Flynn," a voice repeated. "She made it out."

Then the crowd outside the wall was moving toward me, and I saw Amber frozen in the middle of them, recounting what had happened to one of the reporters gathered there. Fuller was tucked under her right arm, and she stroked his head, trying to calm him down as he yipped at the swirling cameras. When she turned, our eyes met, and from her expression I already knew.

There was still no sign of Reed or Kipps.

EVERYTHING AFTER

37

The lights were hot against my skin. Sara and Charli had tried to warn me about the inevitable sweat fest that would accompany this interview, but I still felt wholly unprepared. I'd borrowed one of Sara's silk blouses. We weren't even three minutes in, and I already had grapefruit-sized pit stains under each arm. Tiny beads ran down the back of my legs. I just wanted it to be over, for everyone to stop looking at me.

"What was that like, knowing you'd been wrongly accused but not being able to do anything about it?" Mario Lopez leaned forward in his chair.

"It was—" Sara started to speak but Arthur Von Appen interrupted her.

"Terrible," he said. "Three years. Three years of my life, gone. I had to change my name and move to this small town in Utah where no one knew who I was. Chrysalis and her team harassed and bullied me. Made up stories about how

I was fired for inappropriate behavior. I couldn't get work."

"You've mentioned that . . ." Mario nodded, but I could tell he was getting annoyed.

Arthur had been living alone for years, isolated from the rest of the world, and I wanted to believe those circumstances were partially responsible for his complete lack of self-awareness. He'd already given three interviews. One to *Our World Now*, this cheesy outlet that usually only did stories about murdered housewives, and another to *Today in America*, where he'd rambled on until they went to commercial to stop him.

"I'm ready to start my life again," Arthur said, adjusting his fedora. "I've been approached about a book deal. I want to get my story out there."

"That's great, Arthur." Amber, ever the producer, clapped, and then the audience started clapping too. That seemed to appease him.

"And you?" Mario looked to Sara and Charli. "What was that like? You were out on bail, listening to all these lies that Chrysalis and the LLP media machine was spewing. I mean, wire fraud. Siphoning money from extras' bank accounts. Those are serious allegations."

"They are." Sara nodded, her hands folded in her lap. "I always held out hope that Jess would be able to help us. That had always been our goal with her returning to the set. We wanted to expose LLP to the public and get Beyond1998's message out to a larger audience."

"It was hard," Charli said. "It came as a surprise to many people, but for Sara and me . . . we've known this for years.

I was scared to even ask to leave, and then thankfully they released us from our contracts."

Mario sat back in his chair. He seemed to enjoy the new role the last several months had created for him. Investigative journalist. Arbiter of justice. He glanced at the script scrolling overhead, then looked down the row at us. Me, Arthur, Sara, Charli, and Amber.

"Jess, you've said you saw proof that LLP was responsible for Rae Lockwood's disappearance."

"I did. I saw footage from that day."

"No one has been able to confirm that," Mario said.

"Chrysalis had it destroyed, I'm sure," I said. "But we're still working on that. I know everyone on Beyond1998 is. Rae deserves to be found."

"Do you think she'll be found alive?" Mario asked.

"I don't know."

I glanced sideways at Sara. We'd hoped, of course, that she was still out there somewhere. But every time I thought of her last few seconds in the parking lot, my body felt empty and cold. If they were willing to do that on camera, what had they done when no one was watching?

"How much of this do you hold Chrysalis personally responsible for? Kiki?" Mario turned to her.

"No one person is completely responsible for the *Stuck* franchise and all the corruption and abuse we've seen. Chrysalis knew everything that was going on inside the set, sure, but she answers to a board. There are the venture capitalists who backed her, many of which she consulted with daily, though they still haven't been held accountable. The other producers have some culpability, too. I was one of the only ones who broke rank those last few weeks of the show, even as it became clear something was really off." Amber recrossed her legs, holding on to her knee. "More people will be implicated, as they should be. This isn't over until more people are held responsible."

"Does it bring you solace, knowing Chrysalis has already been charged? That LLP has gone bankrupt after everything they sunk into a VR experience that never actually went public?" He looked at each of us, waiting for someone to answer. "That the show is, effectively, over?"

"It was upsetting, hearing about what they had planned," Sara finally jumped in. "We're seeing all these really disturbing things inside the set, getting all these reports, and then to find out that they were planning this immersive VR experience? An online marketplace where the audience could move through the set, accruing debt as they went? I mean, who reads the fine details of those terms and conditions pop-ups? Do you think anyone would've known what they were signing up for?"

"Unconscionable." Charli looked at the ground as she said it.

"It is," Mario agreed. "I think that really stunned the fandom, realizing that Like-Life Productions had planned to charge for every minute inside the experience. I don't have to tell you how tough it is out there for a lot of people right now. Jobs are hard to come by. Most houses are uninsurable, with floods and fires and earthquakes becoming more and more the norm. And yet LLP wanted fans inside this world.

A world that would slowly drain their bank accounts—literally indebting them to the show."

"It's all about control," Amber said. "LLP controlled everyone and everything inside the set. This was their way of controlling their audience."

"One last question . . ." Mario's eyes were fixed on me, and I ran my hands over the arms of the chair, bracing myself. "There are obviously people missing here tonight. Jess, it's known that you and Kipps Martin were very much in love. That he was your boyfriend. How does it feel that he's not here with you now? It must be devastating."

"Kipps tried to get out of the set that night," I said. "But he and Reed got caught up in everything that happened. They weren't able to leave until the following week, after all the news broke and Chrysalis was officially charged. They're now back in Pennsylvania with their parents."

I hated having to edit myself. Kipps and his family had lost everything when they left the show, because there were all these weird stipulations in their contracts. It didn't matter if LLP had tried to kill us, because the Martins didn't have fancy lawyers and they didn't have money to fight back. Most of Charli and Sara's savings had been drained in their own legal fight, and any salary I might've made off my episodes hadn't been paid out, and probably never would be. Reed was the one supporting the family for the time being. He was trying to complete his online college degree and work remotely for a news outlet—Kipps said he eventually wanted to become a UX designer, focusing on the ethics behind it.

"Have you spoken to him since?" Mario asked.

"We spoke quickly after, and I was able to tell him I was okay. It's just complicated. He's not eighteen yet. He can't just do whatever he wants."

The last time he'd texted, using Reed's phone, he'd said his parents were talking about doing different *Stuck in the '90s*–related appearances. They were pushing Kipps to make these thirty-second videos for fans. A commercial agent had already reached out to them about being the spokespeople for McCracken's, this restaurant chain where everything came out on conveyer belts. It seemed inevitable that they'd tour and do the convention circuit as a family.

"And what about your parents?" Mario went on.

"I speak to them sometimes. Mostly on social media."

It was weird that our entire relationship had devolved into them commenting on my posts or dropping into my DMs to tell me they were thinking of me. The further away from them I got the more they seemed like strangers, all the emoji hearts between us a cheap substitute for the real thing.

"Your mom and dad are currently on their own press tour. They seem pretty stunned by everything that happened."

"I think they were. They're pretty . . . unaware."

That, at least, was true. I'd watched one of their interviews just last week, and they seemed genuinely confused by what happened with Chrysalis. But, more than anything, by how quickly their media empire had fallen apart. No one wanted to hear my dad's fitness tips, or my mom talking about "overcoming obstacles" when those obstacles had come at other people's expense.

"Well, thank you all," Mario said. "I'm sure this will be

the first interview of many for you."

I smiled, but waited until I was certain the cameras were off before leaning over to Sara. "Unlikely," I said.

"What, you don't like debasing yourself in front of millions?" she whispered.

"It's been fourteen years of that."

We all pulled off our mics. My shirt was practically soaked through, and I had trouble concentrating while trying to make small talk with Mario and all the different producers who'd set the interview up. It had been three months since I left the set. Three months since I'd last seen Kipps, standing at the edge of the intersection, silhouetted by the streetlight.

Of course I missed him. Of course it was devastating, being here and knowing he was hundreds of miles away, and his family was struggling, still trying to make money off the show—or what was left of it.

But for now . . . I just wanted to go home.

38

Since she'd gotten back Sara had moved the computers into our new living room, positioning the screens above the coffee table like a makeshift command center. We had her Zing feed on one, the livestream from the courthouse on another. I went onto the Beyond1998 feed under my real name now, answering questions from ex-fans and confirming whatever details I could. Former extras and producers kept jumping on to provide more stories from inside the *'90s Mixtape* set.

Charli pushed through the front door, her arms loaded with paper bags. I sprang up to help her, and I could feel the soup through the paper, so hot it was hard to hold on to. She stamped the snow off her boots and shook out her knit hat. The winter had been relentless, and the forecast had only predicted more harrowing storms.

"It's the ice age out there," Charli said, her cheeks pink. "I could barely get the truck past Nicholls Road. They haven't cleared anything yet. I think it's just too overwhelming this time." She peeled off her coat. "I will never trust those drones again . . . but they were convenient."

"I kind of miss those spying weasels." Sara was in the middle of a long Zing thread responding to Chrysalis's preliminary hearing. She didn't look away. "Call me weak, but I still have a hard time hating anyone or anything that brings me sushi."

Fuller was curled up on the couch, and he barely acknowledged me as I darted around the kitchen, setting one bag on the counter and taking the second off Charli's hands. Outside, the snow had piled up along the inside of the Illusion Fence we'd had installed, sloping drifts that looked as tall as my head. The three-bedroom cabin was all wood. It felt like an artifact from another time, its floors groaning under our weight. It was hidden off a back road, a perfect private retreat where no one ever bothered us, the forest too dense for drones to reach us. Part of me missed the old house, the rooms where Kipps and I had spent so many months together. But in a way this was easier, not being reminded all the time.

"Whoa," Sara said, turning up the volume. "It's actually happening."

"Chrysalis Remington, the executive producer of *Stuck in the '90s* and its spin-off, *'90s Mixtape*, makes her first appearance in court today," a news anchor said, narrating the scene. "She's been charged with attempted murder in connection with the October tenth crash that nearly killed actors Jessica Flynn and Kipps Martin."

"Actors?" I said. "*Actors?*"

The Beyond1998 feed went off before I could.

ACTORS?? ARE THEY FUCKING KIDDING ME WITH THIS?? a user named Rys11 wrote. *THIS IS AL-READY PISSING ME OFF,* another user added. It was comforting knowing other people saw how twisted it was.

The Beyond1998 feed had over ten million users and was still growing. Every day we were inundated with messages on my social media from people asking who they should contact to tell their own story about LLP. I'd initially thought the night of the crash had changed everything, that having so many people inside the set, seeing what happened with their own eyes, would make it impossible to argue with. But it was really what came after that mattered. Sara's aunt Teresa and I had worked together to get Charli and Sara released from jail, consulting with a lawyer who'd found us through the feed. Former LLP employees came forward to provide information and help prove that neither of them had committed any crimes, that lying, bullying, and manipulation were all straight out of the LLP playbook. Arthur telling his story had helped turn public opinion, too, along with Rae's mom describing the day her daughter had disappeared.

"Sar, your cult just signed on," I said, noticing a few familiar handles on one of the screens. I set bowls of soup on the coffee table.

"They're not a cult." Sara smirked as she said it.

The Beyond1998 feed lit up with activity, moving faster than I could follow. After everything that had happened, Sara had reached hero status. I'd finally been able to go public with what she and Charli had done to help get me out of the set, and that, along with the fact that she'd actually gone to jail trying to take Like-Life Productions down, had made people completely obsessed with her. Charli had been inundated with requests for Sara to do her own separate press tour, or write a book about her experience, but for the time being she'd only made one plan—to go down to Texas in the spring to see her dad's side of the family and meet Teresa in person. It was sweet, seeing how excited Sara got whenever they FaceTimed.

We watched the screens in silence, the captions scrolling under the courtroom scene. Chrysalis looked stricken, her cheeks pale. I'd never realized her hair had been dyed, but now her roots were showing, revealing a two-inch skunk stripe along her center part.

It didn't feel gratifying. Not the way I expected it to. What had happened had still happened, and even though the car crash and some of what she'd said after it had been captured on camera, they still hadn't gotten the evidence they needed to charge anyone from LLP in Rae's disappearance. I spent most days trying to track down the members of the security team who we'd seen in the video, which felt increasingly impossible. I could feel the dread of the coming months, as we tried to help Rae's family get closure. The jury selection and trial would drag out, and we'd all be inundated with requests for interviews, people wanting us to tell these horrible stories all over again.

"I'm exhausted." I pushed the soup container away. "I might go to sleep."

"We don't have to watch this." Charli slid her finger over

the home screen, going back to the menu. "Maybe we can find a movie. Or I think there are cards somewhere . . ."

"It's okay, I'm fine," I said, but I didn't mean it.

"Are you talking to Dr. Dalal tomorrow?" Charli pressed.

"Yeah, why?"

"Just . . . Good. I'm happy to hear that." She hugged me, and I was grateful for how much Charli tried. She was the one who'd encouraged me to call Dr. Dalal back, after she'd left several messages. It turned out she was a well-known psychologist and had been genuinely concerned enough to appear on the show. We'd only talked once, but it did feel better to have someone else to help sort through my thoughts.

"Okay, goodnight for real," I said, and Sara squeezed my hand as I passed her and started down the hall to the bedrooms.

As soon as I got into bed I drew the duvet around my shoulders. I turned off the lights and brought my iPhone into my lap. I scrolled through my texts, lingering on the number I knew was Reed's. I hadn't been completely honest in the interview about how much I'd spoken to Kipps. I could feel his parents watching, waiting to hear if we'd been in contact, and I'd wanted to protect him. Sometimes I'd get a random text from him, a goofy selfie or an audio recording just telling me what he did that day. We'd talked on the phone only a few times, when Reed could cover for him, but it always felt too short.

It meant everything, having Charli and Sara back. Being close to Amber again—genuinely close. I was supposed to visit her in New York City in the spring. But I could still feel it, all the space Kipps had left behind. I'd kept busy and did all the things, but I still had all this love for him and no idea where to put it.

I scrolled up to my favorite video, one Kipps had sent the month after he'd gotten outside the set. He was under his covers, the phone light bright against his skin. His cheek was pressed against a pillow.

"Hey, Jess," he said, his voice barely a whisper. "I just wanted to say hi. And I love you." He was fighting off sleep, his eyes drifting closed. "And I'm thinking about May seventh. And us. And . . . I guess I just wanted to say goodnight."

I played it twice before turning the phone off and clutching it to my chest.

On May seventh, Kipps would finally turn eighteen. As soon as his birthday passed, he wouldn't be tied to his parents, or any of the contracts they'd signed for him. He could do whatever he wanted.

It wasn't that long, I tried to tell myself.

That was only four months away.

ACKNOWLEDGMENTS

So much of the publication process hinges on finding people who get you and get your work, and I'm lucky to have found both with my agent, John Cusick, and my publisher, Quirk Books. John has been a tireless champion for me and for Jess, for which I am very grateful. A huge thank-you to the entire team at Quirk—to Alex Arnold and Jessica Yang, for shepherding this sequel from a few pages to its final draft. To Nicole De Jackmo, Kelsey Hoffman, Christina Tatulli, and Gabrielle Bujak, who've promoted this series with enthusiasm and care. And to Jhanteigh Kupihea, Jane Morley, Andie Reid, Elissa Flanigan, and Kassie Andreadis, who have all made these books better in different ways. Thank you for responding with a resounding *YES!* when I proposed returning to Swickley.

As always, gratitude to my friends and family, but especially to Robin Wasserman, who was sent an eleventh-hour draft which she miraculously read in a few days. Writers out there know how rare that is. Love and gratitude to my partner, Clay, for seeing me (and my grumpy self) through a particularly draining first attempt, when I was feeling around in the dark. And most of all, a huge hug and thank-you to you, the reader, for following Jess's story here. From the very first days *This Is Not the Jess Show* was in the wild, I was touched by your bookstagrams and notes, by your passionate reviews and your genuine love for these characters. This is by far my most personal book. There's a lot of *me* in here, making your enthusiasm all the more meaningful. So thank you, again. I wrote this one for you.